Date A Live

Angel Tobiichi

"It's not just Spirits that I'm going to kill. I have to kill the part of me that was swayed by emotion without even realizing it."

Origami Tobiichi
A Wizard who hates Spirits

"You know that Tohka and the others just want to live normal lives, don't you?"

Shido Itsuka
A high school student

"...I'm going to actually try to kill you. Don't die, Origami."

"Origami Tobiichi.
I hate you. I did
before, and I do now.
But my hatred now
is probably...a little
different from the
hatred before. So..."

Tohka
A Spirit

"Origami…Why are you a Spirit now?!"

"Metatron."

Origami Tobiichi
A Spirit

CONTENTS

"Now then,
shall we begin
our date?"

Kurumi
A Spirit

Date A Live
Angel Tobiichi

10

Koushi Tachibana

Illustrated by
Tsunako

YEN
ON

New York

Koushi Tachibana

Translation by Jocelyne Allen
Cover art by Tsunako

DATE A LIVE Vol.10 ANGEL TOBIICHI
©Koushi Tachibana, Tsunako 2014
First published in Japan in 2014 by KADOKAWA CORPORATION, Tokyo.
English translation rights arranged with KADOKAWA CORPORATION, Tokyo through TUTTLE-MORI AGENCY, Inc., Tokyo.

English translation © 2023 by Yen Press, LLC

Yen On
150 West 30th Street, 19th Floor
New York, NY 10001

Visit us at yenpress.com
facebook.com/yenpress
twitter.com/yenpress
yenpress.tumblr.com
instagram.com/yenpress

First Yen On Edition: October 2023

Edited by Yen On Editorial: Ivan Liang
Designed by Yen Press Design: Andy Swist

Yen On is an imprint of Yen Press, LLC.
The Yen On name and logo are trademarks of Yen Press, LLC.

Library of Congress Cataloging-in-Publication Data
Names: Tachibana, Koushi, 1986– author. | Tsunako, illustrator. | Allen, Jocelyne, 1974– translator.
Title: Date a live / Koushi Tachibana ; illustration by Tsunako ; translation by Jocelyne Allen.
Other titles: Dēto a raibu. English
Description: First Yen On edition. | New York, NY : Yen On, 2021–
Identifiers: LCCN 2020054696 | ISBN 9781975319915 (v. 1 ; trade paperback) |
    ISBN 9781975319939 (v. 2 ; trade paperback) | ISBN 9781975319953 (v. 3 ; trade paperback) |
    ISBN 9781975319977 (v. 4 ; trade paperback) | ISBN 9781975319991 (v. 5 ; trade paperback) |
    ISBN 9781975320010 (v. 6 ; trade paperback) | ISBN 9781975348298 (v. 7 ; trade paperback) |
    ISBN 9781975349943 (v. 8 ; trade paperback) | ISBN 9781975350307 (v. 9 ; trade paperback) |
    ISBN 9781975350321 (v. 10 ; trade paperback)
Subjects: GSAFD: Science fiction. | Fantasy fiction.
Classification: LCC PL876.A23 D4813 2021 | DDC 895.63/6—dc23
LC record available at https://lccn.loc.gov/2020054696

ISBNs: 978-1-9753-5032-1 (paperback)
        978-1-9753-5033-8 (ebook)

10 9 8 7 6 5 4 3 2 1

LSC-C

Printed in the United States of America

Spirit

A uniquely catastrophic creature existing in a parallel world. Cause of occurrence and reason for existence unknown. Creates a spacequake and inflicts serious damage on her surroundings whenever she appears in this world. A very powerful fighter.

Strategy No. 1

Annihilate with force. This approach is very difficult, since the Spirit is extremely powerful, as noted above.

Strategy No. 2

...Date her and make her all weak in the knees.

Angel Tobiichi

Spirit No. 1
Astral Dress—Angel Type
Weapon—Crown Type [Metatron]

Prologue
Origami Tobiichi

It was about five years ago that the girl known as Origami Tobiichi became "special."

She'd always gotten excellent grades at school and displayed impressive athletic skills, but this sort of excellence wasn't anything outrageous. At most, it allowed her mother to hold her head high at PTA meetings and parent-teacher interviews.

Her best subject was arithmetic, and her worst was language arts. Her favorite food was potato gratin, and her least, celery. When she grew up, she wanted to be a beautiful bride.

The world was filled with common sense and customs that no one questioned. When Origami did things that she found natural, friends and grown-ups patted her head and praised her. She assumed that the world would always be this kind to her.

But one summer day five years ago changed everything.

What greeted her when she came home that day was not her familiar neighborhood, but a scene straight out of hell wreathed in raging crimson flames.

Mom, Dad…

She remembered her parents were supposed to be home and ran straight toward the fire.

This was an extremely reckless act. There wouldn't have been much she could have done even if she had made it to her house. But in that moment, Origami couldn't think of anything other than making sure her parents were okay.

Before too long, she was standing at the gates, watching her father kick down the door of their burning house and rush outside, his arm wrapped around her mother's shoulders.

Words could not express Origami's relief in that moment. Her parents were alive. She was utterly overjoyed, tears welling up in her eyes as she reached out to take her father's hand.

But in the next instant, a beam of light fell from the sky.

"Huh?"

Origami was knocked into the air, like a feather on the wind.

And her parents, who had been standing where the blinding beam struck the ground, had been blown apart into such tiny fragments that it was almost impossible to believe they had been people seconds earlier.

"Ah... Ah... Aaaaaaah!"

Gnashing her teeth so hard that they groaned, Origami looked up at the sky.

There, she saw the silhouette of the girl who had shot the deadly ray of light.

"You...

"Mom. Dad.

"You won't get away with this! I'll kill you... I swear I'll kill you! That's a promise...!"

Origami vowed to exact her revenge in a voice filled with hatred.

That was her first encounter with the Spirits, the starting point that tied their fates together.

Origami changed after that day.

Because she had no other family, she was taken in by an aunt who lived nearby. And this aunt was a former member of the AST, a fact that determined the subsequent course of Origami's life. Her aunt told her of the existence of beings that were a secret from the public at large: Spirits. World-killing catastrophes.

From that point on, Origami devoted herself completely to her studies and training to an almost alarming degree. All her effort was for one reason and one reason alone: to hunt down the Spirit she saw that tragic day and get her revenge.

Of course, at such a young age, Origami didn't know exactly how to go about actually making this happen. Instead, she trained incessantly, frantically, desperately to ensure that she would be ready the instant she discovered who had killed her parents. She pushed her mind and body so hard that she almost seemed more like a merciless devil or an angry demon than a child.

Her best subject was…everything. Her worst, nothing in particular. She mastered every field and every skill she came across and repeatedly flouted the concept of *impossible*. She had not differentiated between favorite and least favorite foods since that fateful day. Her only concerns were obtaining the required nutrition that would build a strong body, and she paid no attention to anything else. As she grew up, killing that Spirit was her only desire.

A few years later, after a formal introduction from her aunt, Origami stood at the doors of the AST. Her compatibility with the Realizer was immediately obvious, so she was quickly inducted into their ranks as a Wizard. Once she joined up, her training grew even more intense.

The world was filled with nonsense and contradictions that no one ever questioned, never mind resisted. Origami knew she would never be able to achieve her objective on her own. The only way to survive in this cruel world was to stay laser-focused on her sole reason for living.

But as steely as she was, even Origami had something that made her feel at peace.

For her, it was a boy she met that day.

Thinking back, her feelings might have been less adoration and more dependence after losing both of her parents. She leaned on this boy and just barely managed to keep herself whole. Which was why even though he was the main reason she had been kicked out of the AST, she did not and could not resent him.

When she thought about it now, she realized that perhaps it was also because she had gone as far as she could there. The AST had been formed with the objective of defeating the Spirits, and the Realizers gave human beings supernatural powers. But even then, the AST was still far from being close to a match for the Spirits.

So she sought greater strength.

The company that produced the Realizers, DEM Industries...they could provide her the most cutting-edge equipment and a body that could use it.

Then Origami...

Chapter 1
Shido in the Crosshairs

The first oddity he noticed in the darkness was the smell. The fragrance reminded him of soap or flowers. The scent tickling his nostrils clearly wasn't coming from himself.

"Mm…" Groaning slightly, he twisted around and stretched.

Then he felt a gentle warmth pressing up against the back of his hand.

"Eek!"

He heard a quiet squeal.

"Huh?" He forced the last dregs of sleep from his head and sat up, rubbing his eyes.

The first thing he saw was his own bed. Crumpled blankets lay on white sheets. But these were clearly not what his hand had bumped against. Not to mention the fact that a blanket couldn't speak.

He slowly opened his eyes.

"Heh-heh… Morning, Shido." A woman in her underpants snuggled up next to him and smiled bewitchingly as she sensually brushed her hair back.

She looked to be in her midtwenties, with long, slender limbs and an ample bosom. Her beautiful, perfectly proportioned face would have put many a model to shame.

"…Mm. Yeah. Morn—," Shido started to respond, sleep still weighing down his eyes, and then he froze.

"Wh-whaaaaaaaat?!"

The second his brain registered that this was no regular morning occurrence, he pulled back to try and get some distance. Unfortunately, he was on his bed. With nowhere for his feet to go and his butt sliding over the edge, he tumbled backward and hit his head on the floor.

"Ngah!" he cried.

"Oh my! You really must be more careful, Shido."

Her giggling filled the room as he raised his head and looked up at the bed in bewilderment and shock.

"N-Natsumi?!" he shouted, completely baffled. "Why are you—?"

Shido knew exactly who this was. How could he forget the Spirit whose power he had sealed just the other day?

"Why? I'm here to say hello, of course. I came to wake up the sleeping prince." She sat up slowly and stretched, the simple move instantly becoming a scene out of a movie when she performed it. "Mmm!"

Shido was nearly drawn in by the gorgeously languid gesture, but he quickly recovered and shook his head vigorously from side to side.

"No, not that! Wait, I mean, I am also curious about why you're sleeping here, but more importantly..."

He rubbed his eyes again, pinched his cheeks, and checked that he wasn't actually still asleep before continuing:

"...Natsumi, why are you a grown-up?!"

According to his memory, this beauty was not Natsumi's true form, but rather the ideal woman that she turned into when she used her Spirit power of transformation.

But Shido had locked away Natsumi's powers. She shouldn't have been able to use that ability. Even the limited use of Spirit power only became possible when the Spirit's mental state was incredibly unstable.

Did that mean Natsumi was under intense stress at the moment? From the look of her, though, she didn't seem to be all that upset.

While Shido was considering the various possibilities, the door to his room swung open.

"What is all the ruckus in here?!" A girl in her early teens stepped inside, hair pulled up into pigtails with black ribbons. Shido's little sister, Kotori Itsuka, had evidently grown suspicious of the yelling and the loud *thump* of his fall, compelling her to come to take a look.

"...So." Kotori surveyed the room, one of her eyebrows shooting up as her gaze moved from Shido on the floor to the half naked Natsumi. And then despite the fact that Shido could see her underpants from this angle, she swung a leg up into the air and dropped her heel squarely on his stomach. "What are you two up to first thing in the morniiiiiing?!"

"Gyan!" Shido doubled over and writhed on the floor, holding his stomach.

Kotori used the momentum of her kick to whirl around, turned her back to him, and stomped on the floor before thrusting her left palm forward and throwing out her right fist for a big finishing pose. If this were a fighting game, KO! would have no doubt popped up in between the two of them.

"Hmph. 'Gyan'? Maybe you should consider a career in antiques?"

"Y-you..." Shido raised a voice in protest, but Kotori appeared supremely uninterested.

"And what on earth were you thinking? Attempting to commit your lechery in the same house as your little sister? I thought you had a little more judgment and discretion than that."

"This is a frame job!" he cried.

"Whoa, a frame job." Kotori shook her head. "Sounds kinky."

"Don't be so literal! Anyway, for some reason, Natsumi was lying down next to me when I woke up."

Kotori turned a dubious gaze on Natsumi. "She was?"

Natsumi's cheeks reddened, and she hugged herself as she opened her mouth awkwardly. "Shido's...a pervert."

"...!"

Kotori's gaze sharpened, and she raised a foot once more to drop her heel on Shido. This time, he managed to catch it just before impact.

"C-calm down!" he shouted in his defense. "I seriously didn't do anything!"

"...For real, right?"

"F-for real! And how come Natsumi can change into her adult version?" he asked. "Did something happen?!"

"Ohhh." Kotori slowly brought her foot back down to the floor. "Now that you mention it, I guess I didn't tell you, huh? About Natsumi's status."

"Status?" he said nervously. "What do you mean? You're not saying the seal was incomplete, are you?"

"No." Kotori lowered her eyes and shook her head. "The seal itself was a success. Natsumi's Spirit powers are definitely locked away inside you, the same as with the other Spirits."

"So then something's disturbing her mental state?!"

"Mmm." Kotori groaned, a complicated look on her face. "When you put it that way... Sort of. More or less."

"Hmm? Meaning...?" He frowned. Not a single bit of this made any sense.

Perhaps concerned about Natsumi overhearing her, Kotori bent down and brought her face close to his ear. "Natsumi's not exactly the most stable, mentally speaking, remember?"

"Ohhh." Shido scratched his cheek thoughtfully, still lying on the floor in an unnatural position. Now that she mentioned it, pretransformation Natsumi was a bundle of neuroses and complexes, and her mood could deteriorate at the drop of a hat.

"Basically," Kotori told him, "Natsumi has a way easier time manifesting her abilities than Tohka and the others."

"I-isn't that pretty dangerous?" he stammered.

"Mm. At the moment, though, the only power she can use is changing her own appearance, so I'm thinking we'll just leave it be for now. This is the look she naturally reaches for to hide when she's embarrassed or doesn't want to be seen. All we can do is let her get comfortable living in her own skin over time."

"Y-yeah?"

"Heeey, what are you two whispering about? Let me join in," Natsumi said, pulling her tousled hair together in an excessively suggestive manner. She seemed so bold and unflinching. Nothing hinted at a fragile state of mind. Whenever she transformed into her older form, her personality also changed. She was brimming with so much confidence that it seemed like she was literally a different person.

"Natsumi, listen up." Kotori stood up with a sigh and rolled her eyes. "It's all fine and good to wake Shido up for me, but you gotta do something about this habit of transforming yourself at the drop of a hat. You keep going like this, and you'll never be able to blend into society."

"Aww." Natsumi raised her eyebrows in a show of concern. "Don't go getting *angwy* that I took your job of waking Shido up. You'll ruin that pretty face of yours."

"Th-that's not what we're talking about right now!"

"Hee-hee! You don't have to say it. It's written all over your face. And, Kotori, with that body of yours, you can snuggle up against Shido while he's sleeping all you want, but he might not even notice you." Natsumi crossed her arms under her breasts, practically announcing their size.

"Wh-what?!" Kotori cried out, indignant.

"I meeean, it's true, isn't it? I can see a certain amount of demand for this sort of thing, but it lacks some firepower. Or more like, you're *so* aerodynamic that people could call you a work of art."

"Ngh! Don't underestimate me! I'm still developing, all right?!"

"Whaaat?" Natsumi frowned. "But your breasts stop developing when you're around fifteen, you know?"

"I-I'm only fourteen!" Kotori snapped in response. "And, like, who are you to talk anyway?! You might have a hot bod because you're transformed, but *you're* actually the shrimp here!"

"...!"

The look of utter confidence on Natsumi's face turned into shock. Shido felt like darkness had suddenly descended over the room. If this were a manga, a sound effect like *bam* or *whump* would have appeared above Natsumi's head.

"I—I knew it." Natsumi covered her face with her hands, and her shoulders began to shake. "So that's what you think, Kotori. Ungh. Ungh, ungh… I'm so stupid. I got all excited, I thought I'd made a friend…even though there's no way anyone could actually accept me…"

Everything clicked for Shido. Natsumi's confidence crumbled like tofu.

The look on Kotori's face said that she'd really stepped in it, and she hurried over to Natsumi.

"Th-that's not what I think," she said. "I was just reacting without thinking. Like you were picking a fight, and I was taking you up on it."

"Ungh! Ungh!" Natsumi cried. "It's okay, Kotori, you don't have to pretend to care. I'm sorry you have to put up with me… I'm sorry for getting so full of myself when I have zero reason to…"

"No, seriously! I really don't think that!"

"But…I *am* shrimpier than you, Kotori…"

"Y-you're not, though?!"

"…So then you're shrimpier than me?"

"Urk! Th-that's…," Kotori stammered, sweat beading on her forehead.

Fat tears welled up in Natsumi's eyes, and she began to sob in earnest. "I knew it was a lie! A gentle lie that hurts the heart the moooost!"

"Aww…! Come on! Yes, fine! I'm shrimpier!" Kotori said finally, abandoning all hope.

Natsumi stopped crying on the spot, as if there had never been any tears, and began to laugh and clap her hands. "Ah-ha-ha-ha-ha-ha! You're shrimpy! Kotori's so shrimpyyyy!"

"Wha—?" Kotori looked completely baffled, like she couldn't even process what had happened. But she quickly regained her composure, and her eyes became sharp, thin lines as she glared at Natsumi. "Y-you…you tricked me?!"

"Eek! The shrimp's attacking me!" Laughing innocently, Natsumi leaped up from the bed, left the room, and raced downstairs.

"Hey, you! Stop right there!" Kotori chased after her, stomping down the stairs.

And then at last, there was peace in Shido's room.

"Guess I'll wash my face." He let out an exasperated sigh before slowly pulling himself to his feet.

Although he had gotten a surprise upon waking, the rest of his morning was almost shockingly routine. He washed his face, got dressed, had breakfast with Kotori—who'd failed to catch Natsumi—and stepped outside.

"Shido!"

He heard a cheerful voice coming from the condo next door. He looked over to find a girl in the Raizen High uniform, waving a hand energetically.

With long hair the color of the night and distinctive eyes that glittered like crystals, she was almost too beautiful. Couple those with her cute button nose and lips like sakura petals, anyone who laid eyes on her must have felt like they were gazing upon one of the sacred mysteries of the world. But the expression on this lively face was a smile so bright and friendly that they immediately overwrote that impression in an instant.

Tohka Yatogami. Neighbor to the Itsukas and Shido's classmate.

"Hey, Tohka." Shido waved back. "Morning."

"Mm. It's morning!" Tohka bobbed her head up and down, her smile stretching from ear to ear. Her every move was filled with happy energy. As always, this was a girl who lived to the fullest. "The weather's amazing today, too! All nice and warm!"

"Yeah, hard to believe it's November. Hey, where are Kaguya and

Yuzuru? They oversleep again?" Shido craned his neck and looked behind Tohka. He could see no sign of Kaguya and Yuzuru Yamai, who lived in the same building as Tohka.

"No, they left already," Tohka told him. "I guess they were having a contest to see who could make it to school first today."

"Oh, they were?" Shido couldn't help but smile wryly at their usual antics. Kaguya and Yuzuru were extremely close, but they liked contests more than eating breakfast and lunch (he wanted to say breakfast, lunch, and dinner, but apparently, missing three whole meals would get in the way of their competitions), and they would challenge each other on the flimsiest of pretexts.

"Okay, should we get going?" he asked.

"Mm!" Tohka agreed enthusiastically.

They began to walk down the familiar road to school. This, too, was an utterly normal moment. The same old, same old. One more step in the daily grind that had repeated over and over and over these last few months. These peculiar beings known as Spirits, an extraordinary existence that far surpassed the realm of the everyday, had at some point become an intimately familiar part of his life.

"Ow, ow." Shido looked up at the sky abruptly and grimaced at the sharp pain he suddenly felt in his neck.

"Mm?" Tohka looked at him with concern. "What's the matter, Shido?"

"Aah... I kind of fell out of bed this morning."

"Mm. You have to be careful."

Shido smiled at her reassuringly. "I don't usually fall out of bed. Today, Natsumi—" He cut himself off hurriedly.

"Natsumi?" Tohka frowned. "Is something wrong with Natsumi?"

"Oh! Uh. No, forget it." He waved a hand in an attempt to quickly move on.

Tohka looked at him curiously, but then her eyes opened wide as though she had just remembered something. "Right! Speaking of Natsumi, something's been bugging me."

"Hmm? What's that?"

"Is her name Natsuumi because she's loved by everyone?"

"Ohhh." His relief at the change of subject was fleeting. Faced with this question, he felt sweat beading on his face. *Natsuumi* was a word he had taught Tohka. It meant "I love you"…but this was actually just a thing he made up to distract Tohka when he accidentally called her Natsumi. "R-right. A word that means 'I love you' or 'you're the best' is pretty great, after all. People make names out of words like that all the time. Like, you know, Yamabuki in our class, her name's Ai, right? That also means 'love.'"

"Oh! I get it!"

Shido kept spinning out the lie, and Tohka clapped like that resonated deeply with her. He felt his own heart throb painfully. Yamabuki did not spell her name with the character for "love," but with something entirely different. It *was* a homophone, though.

As they walked and talked, they reached the high school before too long. They changed into their indoor shoes like always, climbed the stairs like always, entered the classroom like always, and sat down at their desks like always. Shido's was the second from the window, and Tohka's was the one to his right. For some reason, he felt like his classmates were shooting guarded glances at him the second he entered the classroom, but well, he decided that was probably all in his head.

The only thing he had to do now was get ready for the upcoming lesson and chitchat with Tohka some more about nothing important. This, too, was no different from the usual.

However.

"…"

Silently, he looked at the desk to his left. A desk where no one was seated. The desk of his classmate, Origami Tobiichi.

Yes. There was one element missing from his usual, every day.

"Origami," he said quietly.

"Mm…" Perhaps overhearing this, Tohka also turned her gaze toward Origami's desk.

Origami was a member of the AST, the group whose stated objective was the annihilation of the Spirits. Naturally, Origami and Tohka were definitely not on particularly good terms. In fact, it might have been more apt to say that they fought like cats and dogs.

But for some reason, Shido felt like Tohka's eyes contained a complicated mix of emotions when she looked at the empty desk.

Perhaps that was also only to be expected. Shido nodded slightly as he let out a sigh and thought back on the last time he'd seen Origami.

A few days earlier, Tengu had been plunged into crisis when DEM Industries tried to drop an orbital satellite equipped with explosive technology onto the city. Shido and the Spirits had, with the help of Ratatoskr, managed to stop it at the very last second, but DEM Industries had kept one last trick up their sleeve. They released a bomb with the same explosive force as that of the satellite from an airship over Tengu. Their power completely exhausted, Shido and the Spirits were caught off guard. They were completely out of options.

That was when a Wizard appeared from the sky above and detonated that bomb with a single blow.

Origami.

"What *was* that?" Shido muttered to himself and pressed a hand to his forehead as his thoughts raced.

Normally, he could have explained the whole thing away as Origami helping them out of a jam, end of story. He could just throw his hands up in the air in celebration and thank her from the bottom of his heart.

However, he felt like it wasn't actually that simple.

The CR unit Origami had been wearing wasn't her usual SDF AST regulation equipment, but rather something from DEM Industries. What exactly did that mean? At the end of it all, Origami hadn't descended to greet Shido and the Spirits. She'd only given them a meaningful look before flying off somewhere. He'd thought he could simply ask her for the whole story the next time he saw her, but...

A familiar chime played over the classroom speaker.

"Time for homeroom, huh," he said absently.

The students who were scattered in and outside the classroom hurried to find their seats. Shido glanced at the window and caught sight of several boys and girls slipping through the closing school gates. But Origami was indeed not among them.

"Maybe she's out sick today?" He sighed quietly. It was a sigh of dejection and the tiniest bit of relief.

Still, he was going to have to deal with this at some point. Maybe it would be a good idea to stop by Origami's condo on the pretext of checking in on her on his way home today.

While Shido was considering this, his homeroom teacher, Tamae Okamine aka Tama, entered the classroom.

Stand, bow, sit.

Once the students had finished the usual greeting, Tama opened her class ledger.

"Okay, good morning, everyone. Let's have a great day!" For all the "great" talk, Tama sounded relatively somber as she let her eyes drop to the ledger.

His classmates started giving looks to one another at this very un-Tama-like gloom.

"Uh. Is something wrong with Tama?"

"She seems kinda bummed."

"Oh! Maybe she had another matchmaking fall through."

"Ohhh…"

Whispers of pure speculation flew.

Whether Tama could hear these or not, she let out a long sigh.

"Before I take attendance, I have some sad news for all of you," Tama said, her eyebrows pulling up on her forehead into a concerned arc.

At this ominous statement, various members of the class murmured, "I knew it."

"I *told* her she put too much effort into her matchmaking photos."

"I mean, I know that if you don't make a good first impression, potential matches might not even meet with you. But if the difference is too huge, then the whole thing's off anyway, y'know?"

"But would she actually go and announce that during homeroom?"

"Huh? So what could it be?"

"What if she got catfished and they took everything she had?"

"Whoa. Now *that's* sad."

Speculations came from every mouth.

Tama coughed rather deliberately to chide the rumormongers and then continued speaking. "The truth is…though a sudden turn of events, Tobiichi has transferred to a new school."

"What?!" Without even thinking, Shido leaped to his feet.

Tohka also opened her eyes wide in surprise.

Everyone in the class looked shocked, but even still, Shido's reaction was over-the-top. All eyes turned to him.

Normally, this would be very uncomfortable for him. But right now, Shido didn't have the extra mental energy to even notice it. He slammed his hands onto his desk and lobbed questions at Tama.

"W-wait just a second! Origami? Origami transferred?! What exactly happened?!"

"I—I know it's a surprise," Tama said. "I don't know the details myself. We got this phone call from Tobiichi saying that she was transferring and would send the necessary papers later."

"That's…" Unable to hide how shaken he was, Shido pressed a hand to his forehead.

Around him, his classmates began to whisper again. Most likely, they hadn't expected him to be this upset. If anything, they were maybe more shocked that Shido hadn't heard about this from Origami herself.

"S-so then…exactly which school did she transfer to?" Shido continued, grasping at straws. If he knew the name of the school, he could easily get Ratatoskr to look into this whole thing.

His desperation apparently touched Tama. She hurriedly dropped her eyes to the sheet of paper tucked into the class ledger and then lifted a face colored with confusion. "W-well, you see, that... I-it just says a school in England."

"...!"

Shido swallowed hard.

"Ungh... Ungh, unhgaaaaaah!" Natsumi was screaming into a pillow in an apartment in the building next to the Itsuka house.

She kicked and flailed and beat the bed, paying no mind to the dust this kicked up and occasionally twisting and writhing at the embarrassing, awkward memory of what happened earlier that day. It was almost like she'd been possessed by a demon or turned into a high school boy whose mother had found his special treasures beneath his bed.

"Ugh. Hnnngh."

After a few minutes of this, Natsumi flopped down face-first, utterly spent.

This wasn't to say her spirit was spent, however. She was just physically exhausted from moving so much.

She lay there for a bit until she recovered enough to slowly pull herself up and look at the mirror on the wall. There, she saw the gloomy face of a shrimpy, lanky girl. At the very least, there wasn't any trace of the sexy, attractive older woman who'd been snuggling with Shido.

This was Natsumi's true form.

"Aaah. Honestly, why am I like this?" She ran anxious hands through her hair and once again threw herself down on the bed.

But Natsumi didn't hate her true form the way she once had. She would've been lying if she said she had absolutely no complaints, of course. If only she was a little taller, her chest a little larger—the list of things that she found unsatisfactory was endless.

But her image of herself had greatly improved in a very short amount of time. She was gradually starting to accept her true form, which she had once hated to the point of absurdity. And it was all thanks to Shido and the Spirits. They had "transformed" Natsumi, and more than anything else, they accepted her.

She was very grateful to them. Which was exactly why she'd been mulling over how to pay them back in her own way. This had led to her getting up early, thinking that she could help everyone else rise and shine.

Things hadn't gone exactly according to plan.

Sneaking into Shido's room to start was all fine and good. But the moment she'd gone to wake him up, a strange nervousness had come over her.

What was she supposed to say when he asked why she was there after she woke him up? Well, the natural answer to that was obviously that she came to wake him up. But there was the possibility that he would follow this up with another "why." In fact, it would still be fine if it simply stopped there. But if Shido was the kind of person to wake up grumpy, then there was the chance that he would get mad at her.

Wait, wait, wait. More importantly, what if...?

While all these thoughts ran through her head, Shido abruptly groaned and rolled over. That was when Natsumi hit maximum nervousness. Before she knew it, she had transformed into the supposedly sealed adult version of herself.

Curiously, even though it was just her appearance that had changed, she felt strangely calm, almost like she discovered a whole new kind of confidence in that form. Things she found impossible to do as herself became laughably easy. To be more specific, she could strip down to her underclothes, crawl into bed with Shido, and set up a morning surprise for him. Or fake-cry at Kotori and trick her. That kind of thing.

After she'd fled from Kotori and returned to her own apartment, Natsumi laughed for a bit before returning to her original form.

"Ngaaah…" And now here she was, plunged into the depths of extreme self-loathing. She hated how weak she was. So sick of this sickliness. The softest tofu was a million times stronger than she was.

Out of nowhere, the doorbell rang, and Natsumi jumped. From the sound of it, it wasn't the buzzer in the building's lobby, but rather the doorbell at the front door of her apartment.

She was so surprised, she very nearly turned into an adult again. She pressed a hand to her chest to calm her pounding heart. Then she took a few deep breaths and walked toward the front door, taking care to tread lightly.

For a second, she thought Shido or Kotori had chased her all the way to her apartment, but they should have already been at school. So then who on earth…?

"Wh-who is it?" Natsumi asked ever so timidly, standing in front of the door (but too scared to actually look through the peephole).

While the doors of this condo were quite sturdy in preparation for any eventuality, they were also equipped with mics and speakers just like an intercom, so it was possible to speak directly through them.

Before too long, someone responded in a quiet voice. "Oh, um. It's Yoshino."

"And Yoshinon!"

"…?!" Natsumi furrowed her brow.

Naturally, she knew who this was. Yoshino was a Spirit like Natsumi—they also lived in the same building.

What on earth could she want? Natsumi craned her head curiously to one side as she reached for the doorknob.

But then she caught sight of herself in the mirror on the shoe-closet door and gasped. She had been flailing about on her bed until that very minute, and her hair, which she had so carefully combed that morning, was a total mess. It looked like she hadn't bothered to so much as pat it into place. Maybe it was an issue with the texture of her hair; the moment she let her guard down, it would explode.

"H-hang on!" she called.

"Huh? O-okay."

After hearing Yoshino's reply through the door, Natsumi trotted down the hallway to the washroom and dragged a large brush through her hair.

"G-great!"

Three minutes later, she set the brush down and ran back to the front door. The results of the brushing were naturally far from perfect, but it was the best she could do on such short notice. At a bare minimum, she had at least managed to somehow tame her horrific bedhead.

Natsumi took a deep breath and opened the door.

The small girl standing there bowed neatly. "Um. Good morning, Natsumi."

She was very adorable, wearing a newsboy cap with a cute design and a rabbit puppet on her left hand. Her slightly wavy hair was blue like the ocean, and her eyes glittered like sapphires.

"G'mornin', Natsumiiii! How ya doing?" The puppet also greeted her with a deft movement. This was Yoshino's friend, Yoshinon.

"Ah... M-morning...," Natsumi replied, averting her eyes the tiniest bit. If she'd been in her adult form, she could've said something like "Morning, Yoshino! Yoshinon! What on earth's going on? Did you maybe miss me? Aww, how sweet!" Then she might even throw in a hug. But for the current Natsumi, the bar for that was far too high.

For a moment, there was silence.

What exactly was she supposed to do? Yoshino had come all the way over here, so someone who had their act together would probably have invited her in, saying something like "We can't chat standing in the doorway, come on in. I have some nice tea." But if Yoshino's errand was minor enough that it could be taken care of right away, then asking her in would actually put Yoshino in an awkward position. It would end up with Yoshino having to come all the way inside and have tea, only to be finished with what she came for in a few words. Others might have suggested they could just enjoy a nice chat, but only someone who was a god of communication would ever assume talking with people was a total breeze, or so Natsumi thought. And if she could do that, then Natsumi wouldn't have been stuck here standing awkwardly in the entryway of her apartment. Plus, she didn't even know which, if any, of the many teas in her kitchen were decent.

Yoshinon flapped its mouth while Natsumi was agonizing over the possibilities, sweat beading on her forehead. *"Hey, so, Natsumi? If we stay here forever like this, it'll be a whole thing, y'know? Maybe we could come in?"*

The most perfectly timed lifeboat. *This* was someone who had their act together, unlike Natsumi.

"Y-Yoshinon...!" Yoshino said, as if chiding the puppet.

Natsumi hurriedly shook her head. "I-it's okay. Come in. I don't have much, but..."

"Sorry, Natsumi..."

"I—I said it's totally fine... If anything, I wanted to ask you to come in," Natsumi said, the pitch of her voice growing higher, and gestured Yoshino and Yoshinon into the apartment.

After bowing once more, Yoshino took off her shoes, lined them up neatly in the entryway, and stepped up into the apartment. Natsumi's own shoes were scattered to the side where she'd taken them off. Feeling somewhat embarrassed, she quietly reached down to set them side by side.

"S-sit wherever you want. I'll make some tea..." Natsumi pointed Yoshino into the living room before taking a couple of the tea bags that had come with the apartment out of the cupboard, putting them in cups, and pouring hot water over them. There were also proper tea leaves in that cupboard, but she didn't know how to brew them just yet.

She set the cups and some snacks she'd found on the living room table and then sat down across from Yoshino.

"G-go ahead," she told her guest.

"Okay… Thank you." Yoshino dipped her head in a slight bow and took a sip of tea.

Natsumi likewise brought her cup to her lips.

"…"

"…"

Unfortunately, neither Natsumi nor Yoshino found it easy to start a conversation by themselves, so silence reigned once more.

Natsumi tried to give off a vibe of "I can't talk right now because I'm drinking tea" and glanced over at Yoshino. Although she had gone with the flow of things and invited Yoshino in, she wondered why exactly the other girl had come to see her. She couldn't think of a single reason.

"…!"

But then one possibility popped into her head.

Before Shido sealed her Spirit power, Natsumi had dragged Shido and the Spirits into a real uproar. Once it was over, they'd all acted like it was water under the bridge, but it wouldn't have been strange if one or two of them had only pretended to agree with the others while secretly nursing a grudge against Natsumi.

Not to mention that it had been Yoshinon that Natsumi had impersonated. Yoshino's dearest friend. It would have made sense for Yoshino to wait for the moment when Shido and the Spirits were at school to come and get her revenge.

"Um, Natsumi…?" Yoshino said.

"Eep!" Natsumi jumped in her seat and dived under the table. "I-I'm sorry. I…"

Yoshino and Yoshinon cocked their heads to the side, baffled.

"Why are you sorry? Oh! Did you maybe put a little something in Yoshino's tea?!"

"Wh-what…?!"

"Aaah! A sudden sleepiness comes over Yoshino, and she falls to one side. As her consciousness fades, the last thing she sees is Natsumi smiling lustily and licking her lips… Welcome to the wonderful world of yuri!"

"I-I'd never do that!" Natsumi couldn't let this scandalous idea stand. She yanked her head up to protest. But because she had dived under the table, she ended up slamming her head. "Oww!"

"A-are you all right, Natsumi?!" Yoshino asked worriedly.

"Agh... I-I'm fine...," Natsumi replied as she slowly crawled out from under the table. Thanks to Yoshinon, her nerves were a little less tightly wound. She took a deep breath before asking Yoshino, "S-so...! Did...you want something?"

"Umm," Yoshino muttered, like she was having trouble spitting it out, before she averted her eyes, her cheeks coloring faintly. She soon recovered herself, however, and met Natsumi's gaze as she parted her small lips. "It's... Y-you just started living here. So I thought...maybe you don't...know the town so well..."

Here, Yoshino paused to swallow hard, like she was gulping down her nervousness and then continued.

"If you'd like... Just if you want, but I could...maybe...show you around..."

"Huh...?" Natsumi's eyes grew wide at the unexpected words.

"Oh. Um." Yoshino waved her hands in a panic. "I don't know the area super good, either, so maybe I won't be very helpful...but I think I could do a simple tour. Umm, only if it's not a bother..."

"Ungh. Aaah." Natsumi covered her eyes with her hands.

The reason was simple. Yoshino was far too dazzling, and Natsumi could no longer bear looking directly at her.

Although it was only for an instant, she had thought there was a good chance Yoshino had come for vengeance, and she hated this ugly streak she had. She was even starting to feel like the mere act of turning her filthy gaze on Yoshino was an unforgivable act of blasphemy.

"Ngh!" Yoshino frowned, looking troubled. "Uh. Um. I'm sorry. I didn't think you would hate the idea so much..."

"No... That's not it...," Natsumi protested. "It's just like, I dunno, I'm sorry for being born..."

"N-Natsumi...?"

Famous Kinako Sable

Natsumi uncovered her eyes at last, finally able to look at Yoshino properly again. And then she wavered for a moment before saying in a small voice, "Um. So that…that would be great."

"O-okay!" Yoshino cried out happily, an angelic smile spreading across her face.

Seeing this, Natsumi nearly covered her eyes once more.

"But I mean…you'd actually do something like that for me?" Natsumi asked, scratching her cheek. The question was half out of genuine curiosity and half to hide her embarrassment.

Yoshino shrugged slightly. "It's… I'm happy to. Normally around this time, Shido and Tohka and everyone are all at school… Now that you're here, Natsumi, I was hoping…we could talk a lot. And, um…"

She blushed before continuing:

"…w-we're…friends, so…" She squeezed her eyes shut in embarrassment.

Natsumi also flushed red. "Agh! …This girl… Marry me…"

"Whaee?!"

"*Oh-ho?*"

"…!"

Yoshino was so cute that Natsumi had proposed on reflex. This unconscious proposal made Yoshino's shoulders jump up and Yoshinon stroke its chin.

Natsumi shook her head back and forth vigorously. "N-nothing! A-anyway, you'll show me around, right?! Okay, so let's go, let's go right now, let's get going!"

"Ummm…o-okay."

Pushing a bewildered Yoshino before her, Natsumi left the apartment.

"*The number you have dialed is temporarily unavailable. Please try again later.*"

"Hngh." In front of the Raizen High School gates, Shido listened to the recording over his phone and gritted his teeth.

The time was nine thirty. Naturally, school was still in session, but after learning of Origami's sudden transfer, Shido hadn't been able to stay put and do nothing, so he pretended to be sick and left early.

Tohka had looked concerned, but he ultimately decided to leave her at school. He felt like it wouldn't be the best idea to put a Spirit in front of Origami when he didn't know what was happening. As he recalled the DEM CR unit she'd been wearing the last time he saw her, Shido tightened his grip on the phone, which continued repeating the mechanical announcement.

He'd called Origami any number of times since hearing the news in homeroom, but he hadn't been able to get through.

He ended the call, shoved his phone in his pocket, and let out a short sigh.

Regret and helplessness cast shadows across his heart. Origami in DEM equipment... Even after seeing her like that, he'd assumed deep down that Origami of all people would come to school like always. He never imagined that his peaceful slice of life would disappear so suddenly.

"Hngh!" He jerked his face up and started running.

His destination: Origami's condo. He didn't know if she was still there, but even if she wasn't, there might be some clue as to what was going on. At any rate, he had to hurry.

"...!"

Despite the pain in his lungs and the ache in his legs, Shido kept running. He felt like if he moved too slowly, Origami would disappear and be out of his reach forever.

After running for a while, he finally arrived at Origami's condo.

"Haah! Haah!"

When he stopped, the exhaustion and the pounding of his heart that he'd been ignoring hit him all at once. He pressed his hands against his knees and took some deep breaths.

"Please be here…Origami."

He stepped into the lobby with a prayer in his heart and dialed her condo number on the intercom. But no matter how long he let it ring, there was no response. He tried a couple more times, but the result was the same. Had she already said good-bye to the apartment? Or was she just ignoring him?

While Shido was considering this, a woman who apparently lived in the building came through the front door carrying some shopping bags.

"Hup!" He slipped away from the intercom and turned his back to her, pretending to be a resident checking his mailbox.

With practiced ease, the woman punched numbers into the keypad and walked into the building when the automatic door opened.

"…"

Watching this out of the corner of his eye, Shido swallowed hard and waited for the woman to disappear from sight before slipping through the door himself, just as it was on the verge of closing.

"I'm sorry. It's just this one time," he apologized quietly as he walked down the hallway.

He took the elevator up to Origami's floor and came to stand in front of her door.

"Hokay." He nodded to himself and pressed the button of the intercom set up to one side of the door.

Ding-dong. He could hear the sound echoing inside the apartment. But of course, there was no response.

"Origami!" Shido called out and knocked on the door. "It's me. If you're in there, say something."

But he got nothing. He reached out for the doorknob, certain that it was pointless but knowing that he had to try nonetheless.

"Hmm?" He furrowed his brow. The reason was simple. The resistance he'd expected when trying the knob was completely missing. "It's…unlocked?"

A faint ray of light shone into the gloom he'd been on the verge of sinking into. Bracing himself, he pulled harder on the knob, and the door swung open.

"Origami!"

However, the faint hope blooming inside him was instantly trampled by the sight of a completely empty apartment.

"Wha...?"

His eyes flew open in surprise as he kicked off his shoes and entered. He checked the hallway, the living room, and the bedroom, but they were all the same. Not only was there no furniture, but the anti-intruder/anti-escape traps she had so diligently set were also gone. There was no sign that Origami had ever been there. So much so that for a moment, he wondered if he had entered the wrong apartment.

"What is going on...?" Shido cradled his head in his hands and sank lifelessly to the floor.

It wasn't like he hadn't known this was in the realm of possibility. In fact, it had been dancing around in his head as a worst-case scenario the whole time he'd been running here from school. But when reality shoved it in his face, the shock he felt wrenched his heart out of his chest.

"Where... Where did you go, Origami?"

But there was no point in him sitting here and asking that question. He ran his fingers through his hair, put some strength in his legs, and stood up.

And then he set out toward his next destination. Toward a place where he might find some trace of Origami—the SDF Tengu Garrison. Naturally, venturing there was entirely different from visiting Origami's apartment. The SDF Tengu Garrison was a cornerstone of national defense, not to mention the fact that the very existence of the AST itself was hidden from the general populace. The most likely scenario was that they'd turn him away at the gate without hearing a word of what he had to say.

But he had no other ideas. He started walking, clinging to the faintest of possibilities.

However, having determined his next target, Shido ended up stopping short the moment he walked out of the condo lobby.

A girl was standing on the road across from the entrance. Hair long enough to tickle her shoulders, pale skin, an expressionless face with doll-like features.

It was the girl Shido had been looking for, Origami Tobiichi.

"Origami?!" he shouted, and hurried over to her. He grabbed her shoulders. A little too forcefully, but he couldn't help but feel that if he didn't get a good hold on her, she would vanish again in the blink of an eye. "Where on earth have you been?! And what's all this about transferring schools?! Your apartment's empt—"

"…"

Origami silently held up her index finger. And then as if to cut Shido off, she pressed it to his lips and stared at him.

"I want to talk, just the two of us. Come with me," she said quietly. She whirled around, slipped out of his hands, and walked toward the alley.

"Ah! O-Origami!" he called out, but she didn't stop.

She marched steadfastly forward without looking back.

"Ngh…" Frowning a little, Shido slapped his cheeks lightly before going after her. He'd been looking for her to hear what she had to say. There wasn't much he could do besides follow.

But she just kept walking. She steadily moved toward the end of the alley, where there wasn't a soul around.

"C'mon, Origami!" he protested. "How far are you going to go?"

"A little farther," she said, not even glancing back at him, and continued to walk in silence.

"…"

Shido followed, even though he found the whole thing strange. When he turned the nth corner in his pursuit of her, his eyes grew wide as saucers.

"Huh…?"

Origami had turned this corner only a moment before him, and yet there was no sign of her now.

"Origami? Where'd yo—?!"

He gasped as someone had grabbed him from behind, and a handkerchief was pressed over his mouth and nose.

"Wha—? Hey..."

It was all so sudden, he accidentally took a deep breath. A sharp scent assailed his nostrils, and he felt the ground twist under his feet.

"Ungh. Ah..."

Shido's vision swam, and his consciousness faded. His feet gave out, and he collapsed to the ground.

Chapter 2
Radiant Goetia

"You've lost Shido?" Kotori said dubiously, a phone pressed to her ear in her junior high school classroom.

As soon as the bell rang to signal lunch, she got a call from *Fraxinus*. Sensing something ominous, she immediately switched to her black hair ribbons, only to be given alarming information by her staff.

"What exactly does that mean? He's not at school now?"

"No. He's supposed to be, but according to Analyst Murasame, he left early, before first period even started."

"He left early?"

"Yes. We asked Tohka about the incident and learned that Origami Tobiichi had suddenly transferred schools."

"She what?" Kotori frowned. She couldn't believe that Origami Tobiichi would leave without a word to Shido.

She had a few ideas on why Origami would behave so unusually, however. The last time Origami had shown herself to them, she'd been wearing a DEM CR unit. This was the same Origami who had previously fired on DEM forces in order to protect Shido. But Kotori couldn't reject the possibility that Origami had brokered some kind of secret agreement with them. The idea that she had been brain-washed was also not outside the realm of the possible. This was DEM

Industries they were up against. A little brainwashing on their part wouldn't have surprised Kotori in the least.

Most likely, Shido had come to a similar conclusion. Kotori figured he must have gone looking for Origami, unable to just sit back and do nothing.

"That idiot... Without so much as a word to us." Kotori clicked her tongue in annoyance, and continued, lowering her voice so that no one would overhear her. "Losing track of him, with this timing... It stinks to high heaven. Worst case, he's been abducted by DEM. What about Tohka and the Spirits?"

"Tohka, the Yamai sisters, and Miku are on lunch break at school. Natsumi and Yoshino seem to have gone out together."

"Okay. We can't have them getting anxious, but we probably won't be able to keep them in the dark forever. Put everyone we have on this and go after Shido. I'll come back to *Fraxinus* now, too. Whatever it takes, we have to find him before the girls get home."

"Yes, sir!" her subordinate said on the other end of the line.

Kotori ended the call, tucked her phone into her pocket, and pulled her back away from the wall. And then she changed her hair ribbons as she walked over to her friends sitting and eating lunch with their desks pushed together.

"Oh, Kotori! You done with your call?" one girl asked.

"Who was it? Your brother?" followed another.

Kotori gave them a faint smile as she pressed a hand to her stomach and bent over. "Ungh... Unnnngh."

"Wh-what's wrong, Kotori? You okay?"

"Mm. I feel kind of sick," she said weakly. "Sorry, I'm gonna leave early today. Would you tell the teacher for me?"

"Sure, we can do that." Her friend nodded quickly. "But are you okay? Maybe go to the nurse's office?"

"I'm okay. Thanks. I'll see you later." Pained expression on her face, Kotori picked up her bag and shuffled out of the classroom. And headed not for the main entrance, but to the roof.

◇

"…!"

Groaning slightly, Shido slowly opened his eyes.

"Where…?"

His field of vision was hazy. He tried to raise a hand to rub his eyes. And frowned.

He couldn't move his hand. To be more precise, his wrists appeared to be held together behind his back, which explained why his arm refused to come around to the front of his body.

A minute or two later, as his brain gradually woke up, he realized that he had been placed in a chair and his hands were in cuffs. And in a very thorough touch, a rope bound his torso to the chair, while the legs of the chair had been bolted to the floor. It was stubborn workmanship, clearly indicating that whoever did this fully intended to prevent Shido from escaping under any circumstances.

"What the heck *is* this?" Shido muttered absently to himself. Fortunately, he had not been gagged or blindfolded. He slowly swiveled his head to get a bearing on his surroundings.

It was a gloomy space in what looked like the corner of an abandoned building. Cracks ran along the walls, and the ceiling's steel framework was partially exposed. It looked as though a long time had passed since human hands had touched anything around him.

Why on earth was he being held in a place like this? Shido cocked his head to one side at this fundamental question, and then he remembered what had happened right before he lost consciousness.

"Right. I was chasing after Origami," he said, when the door in front of him creaked open.

He whirled his head in that direction to find Origami standing there carrying a large Boston bag.

"Origami! What are you even—?" he started and then gasped. "No way. You're really with DEM?!"

"…"

Silently, Origami walked over to him, set the bag on the floor, and began to root around inside it.

"Wh-what are you...?!" He had no idea what she was going to pull out of that bag, but if she really had gone over to DEM's side, then she was definitely going to do something heinous. Gun, knife, some kind of truth serum... All kinds of possibilities flitted through his head.

However...

"Here."

"Huh...?"

...contrary to his expectations, Origami held out a plastic bottle of mineral water.

"Wh-what's this?" he stammered.

"Water. You're not thirsty?" Origami asked him, totally unfazed by this extremely unnatural situation.

Shido unconsciously furrowed his brow at the discrepancy.

He was indeed thirsty, but he hesitated to drink anything his kidnapper offered him. He eyed Origami and the water with suspicion.

Perhaps noticing this, Origami opened the bottle, took a drink, and made a show of presenting the water in her mouth to him. She was apparently trying to tell him it wasn't drugged.

"..."

"Huh?"

Wait. That wasn't it. She wasn't drinking the water in her mouth; she was coming straight toward Shido with it.

Almost like...she was going to transfer it to his mouth like that.

"S-stop!" he yelped. "I get it! I'll have some! I'll have some, so just let me drink it myself!"

"Ah," Origami said, sounding slightly regretful, after she swallowed. And then she held out the open bottle of water. "Here."

"O-oh. Okay. Slowly— Mrrrngh?!"

Without letting Shido finish, Origami shoved the bottle into his mouth. A forced, secondhand kiss.

Caught off guard and unable to fight back, he gulped down the water that poured into his mouth.

"..."

Origami pulled her hand away, seeming satisfied. And then for some reason, she gave the mouth of the bottle a thorough lick before putting the cap back on.

He was extremely curious about this action, but well, he decided he didn't want to linger on it. He coughed, half choking, before turning his gaze back on Origami.

"So anyway," he said, "I'd like you to untie me."

"I can't do that," Origami replied curtly.

Shido was slightly shaken as he continued. "Ohhh. Fine, I get it. Then could you at least untie the rope and move my hands to my front?"

"I'm sorry." She gave her head a slight shake. "I want you to stay like this a little longer."

"Come on," he pleaded. "I have to go to the bathroom so bad, I'm about to explode. And I mean, you don't want me to just pee my pants here, do you?"

"..."

Without a word, Origami bent over and dug around in the Boston bag. She pulled out another plastic bottle.

For a moment, he thought she was going to make him drink more water even though he'd just told her he needed to go to the washroom. But that wasn't it. He suddenly felt very uncomfortable. There was nothing in the plastic bottle she held in her hand.

She approached him as she opened the empty bottle.

"H-hey...?" he said, sweat beading on his forehead, but Origami didn't stop.

She set the bottle on the floor, put a hand on his belt, and started to take it off, making the buckle rattle.

"Eeeeaaaah! Eeeeeeek!" Having at last figured out what she was up to, Shido twisted his body away, making the chair creak and squeal. "Hey! You know what?! I'm good, actually! I don't have to go!"

"...Oh." Origami tightened his belt back up, an air of chagrin crossing her face.

"Haah... Haah..." Shoulders heaving, Shido took several deep breaths to slow the pounding of his heart before turning back to Origami.

"Origami."

"What?"

"Did you join DEM?" he asked.

"Yes," she replied evenly. She acted so much like this wasn't an issue at all that Shido felt let down.

"That's all you have to say? Do you even know what they're like?"

"More or less."

"So then why—?"

"To get power."

"Power...?" Shido frowned.

Origami began to speak dispassionately. About how, at long last, she had been seriously disciplined for her multiple violations of orders. And how her only option to continue being a Wizard was to join DEM.

"But I mean, it's too dangerous!" he protested when she was done.

"No choice. There's no other way for me to get the power to defeat the Spirits." Origami was quiet, almost surprisingly quiet. Shido found himself unable to say anything in response.

She likely knew much more than he did about DEM Industries. She had already gone through the agonizing and struggling with the decision and thought of every response to all the protests that Shido could possibly come up with. And after so much deliberation, she had chosen this. No rejection. No argument. The only thing Origami's cool voice made him feel was something like a chill.

But Shido couldn't just sit here, overwhelmed. He cleared his throat as if to get back on track and opened his mouth once again.

"So then you kidnapped me on DEM orders, on the order of that Westcott guy?" he demanded. "What exactly are you planning to do to me?"

"..."

Origami shook her head slowly.

"It was my decision to bring you here. DEM knows nothing about this."

"Huh?" Shido was baffled. "What's that mean? Why would you do this, then?"

"I don't actually want to take your freedom from you. I feel bad about that." She averted her eyes as she continued. "It's a last resort. This is the most certain method to keep you from being involved."

"H-hang on a minute. What are you talking about?" Shido asked. "To keep me from being involved? In what?!"

Origami clenched her fists, as though resolving herself anew, before opening her mouth. "In the fight between me and the Spirits."

"Wha—?!" His eyes grew wide as saucers. "S-Spirits? Which Spirits?"

"The Spirits are the Spirits. Naturally." Origami paused for a second and took a breath. "Tohka Yatogami and the others are not exempt."

"…!"

Shido gasped. Despite the fact that he'd only just had some water, his throat was abnormally dry. *Thump, thump.* The pounding of his heart grew louder; he felt like it was shaking his entire body.

Fight the Spirits. And…kill the Spirits.

Now that he was thinking about it, Origami had been saying this since the first time he met her. She had been a member of the AST, whose objective was to defeat the Spirits, so this was only natural. Shido had heard her say something like this any number of times.

And yet for some reason, these words, which should have been far too familiar, were digging painfully into his heart.

"W-wait, Origami!" he said desperately. "You're after the Spirit who killed your parents five years ago, right?! Tohka and the others had nothing to do with that!"

"That doesn't change the fact that they're Spirits," Origami replied coolly. "They're dangerous. To prevent others from becoming just like me, I can't allow them to continue existing."

"Wha—?! Tohka and the others don't even have a Spirit signal anymore! You said that you wouldn't target them in this state—"

"That was the policy of SDF leadership. It doesn't apply now that I'm no longer AST."

"Ngh!" Shido groaned, screwing up his face. She was exactly right.

Origami was saying that she'd obeyed the orders of her superiors even though she disagreed on a fundamental level.

Origami had always been this way. She hated the Spirits, she despised the Spirits, and she wanted to kill the Spirits.

But Shido couldn't help but feel that this was absurdly twisted.

Naturally, a large factor in this was that he didn't want the Spirits and Origami to fight. But even apart from that, he felt something off in Origami's actions.

He somehow managed to suppress the urge to scream and spoke in an extremely calm voice. "Hey, Origami? It's already been more than six months since Tohka transferred to our school, huh?"

"..."

Origami stared at him silently. He felt like this gaze held some meaning that wasn't quite simply that she didn't understand what Shido was getting at.

"Time really flies, right? That Spirit you tried to kill has completely blended into this world now. And of course, it's not just Tohka. Yoshino, Kaguya, Yuzuru, Natsumi, and there's even Kotori and Miku... They're all trying to live as human beings."

Shido continued almost pleadingly.

"Origami. Are you trying to tell me that nothing's changed for you even after being with them and watching them all this time? I mean, the idea that Spirits are Spirits, end of story... How can you say they're so dangerous that the only option is to kill them?!"

"...!"

For the first time since they'd started talking, Origami's expression changed, an eyebrow slightly twitching upward. She walked to one side of the room at a leisurely pace, raised a hand, and punched the wall.

Wham!

"I know all that."

"O-Origami...?"

"Tohka Yatogami, the other Spirits—they're still Spirits. They are targets for revenge. That's how it's supposed to be," Origami said, her voice trembling faintly, and continued as if talking to herself. "I hated how my thinking was changing gradually as I shared a life with them. I swore to get revenge on the Spirits that day five years ago, and yet I was growing accustomed to them and the way things are now. It… scared me."

She slammed her fist into the wall once more.

"The AST disciplinary measures aren't the only reason I joined DEM. It's also because I noticed that I was changing. That I was starting to tolerate a life with Tohka Yatogami in it."

"Wha…?" Shido's eyes flew open, and he raised his voice. "Why… Why is that not okay?! You know that Tohka and the others just want to live normal lives, don't you?"

"No. I can't accept that. Not as long as they're Spirits." She pulled her fist away from the wall and slowly turned her back to him. "It's not only Spirits I'm going to kill. I have to kill the part of me that was swayed by emotion without even realizing it. When I take Tohka Yatogami's life, I will take myself back."

Origami walked out of the room. The door closed with a *slam*, and chunks of plaster crumbled from the wall.

"Stop! Origami! Wait!" Shido called out desperately, writhing in the chair. But he couldn't get out of the well-planned restraints as easily as that.

He wasn't giving up, though. Stuck here like this, he wouldn't be able to stop the fight between Origami and Tohka.

"Dammit! Origami! Origamiiiii!" He shook himself with all the strength in his body and screamed until he was hoarse.

"Are you certain it's wise to allow her to act at her own discretion like this, Ike?" Ellen Mira Mathers said quietly in a suite on the top floor of a hotel in eastern Tengu.

Pale Nordic blond hair, blue eyes. Skin as white as snow, slender limbs. But her aura was not that of the sheltered rich girl her appearance called to mind, but rather that of an experienced warrior.

"Not an issue," the man sitting on the sofa replied in an easy tone, showing no sign of being unnerved by her implacable strength. "I was going to wait and watch a while, it's true. But she's so fired up now. No need to go out of my way to crush the spirit of a bright young Wizard. And we did just go through *that* little ordeal. Took a bit more hush money than usual to get the SDF to take care of things."

He was a young man who seemed to be in his midthirties with dark ash-blond hair and eyes sharp as knives. A deep darkness in his gaze made those who met him feel an unfathomable unease.

Sir Isaac Ray Pelham Westcott. The managing director of DEM Industries, a massive corporation known around the world.

"That *little* ordeal?" Ellen appeared slightly astonished.

And that was really no surprise. Whatever else, Westcott and Ellen nearly had a satellite dropped on their heads a few days ago in a plot schemed up by the DEM board of directors.

Once the details became clear, the members of the board—including the ringleader, Roger Murdock—had been rounded up and arrested back in England, but Ellen was displeased that Westcott still hadn't actually punished them in any tangible way.

Perhaps guessing at this, Westcott shrugged deliberately and continued.

"Naturally, I do not intend to simply abandon our policy thus far. But it's also true that I wish to have a variety of data points. We have all those Spirits just sitting there, after all. We could turn one or two of them into Sefirahs."

A faint smile played on his lips.

"I was actually hoping to get some data of Mordred in live combat. Whatever else, we're up against the Spirits here. And her shooting down a falling explosive doesn't show us the true power of the unit. You also want to see how far she'll go, don't you? Although, well, if her abilities surpass our expectations, then we might have to step in and stop her before she finishes off all the Spirits, hmm?"

Ellen nodded and let out a short sigh.

He was exactly right. She did want to get a grasp on the abilities of this girl Origami Tobiichi.

While they did have records of her achievements and data from her days at the AST, these were, at best, using official AST equipment. How would Origami fare against the Spirits wearing Mordred, DEM Industries' latest CR unit and sister to Ellen's Pendragon? She was indeed interested in studying that. After all, Origami had been scouted to support Ellen on future missions.

"Understood. We'll move behind the scenes this time," Ellen said curtly.

Westcott chuckled. "You seem displeased."

"No, that's not it."

"When you lie, you frown ever so slightly. I can always tell right away, you know."

"…!"

With a gasp, she touched the space between her eyebrows. But there was no noticeable wrinkling there.

"I jest." Westcott smiled merrily.

"…"

Ellen brought her hand back down, a very clear expression of displeasure on her face as she looked at him.

"Ha-ha! Don't be so cross, my dear Ellen. I want you to take up a different target this time."

"A different target?" she asked dubiously.

"Yes." He nodded. "If Origami Tobiichi sets her sights on Princess and the others, there will certainly be interference, yes?"

Ellen's face stiffened. "Ratatoskr."

"Exactly," Westcott agreed.

It was no coincidence that the Spirits had all assembled in this city. They had been placed under the protection of the Spirit-friendly organization Ratatoskr.

And DEM knew that Ratatoskr had an airship to monitor and safeguard the Spirits, respond to spacequakes, and challenge DEM's attempts to annihilate and capture the Spirits.

If Origami Tobiichi went after the Spirits, Ratatoskr would definitely try to stop her. On top of that, former DEM No. 2, Mana Takamiya, was now on Ratatoskr's roster. If she joined in the fray, Origami would have more to worry about than attacking the Spirits.

"You mean to say that I should handle Mana?" Ellen asked, and Westcott slowly shook his head.

"No."

"Then what exactly?"

"I spoke to the head office yesterday. They're sending *Goetia*."

"...!!"

Ellen's eyes grew as wide as saucers at Westcott's words. And then she immediately guessed at his intentions.

"You're telling me to stop Ratatoskr's airship itself?"

"It's incredibly helpful that you're so quick on the draw." The corners of Westcott's mouth pulled up into a grin.

"The mission on Arubi Island, the battle at the Japanese office, the matter with the satellite—Ratatoskr's airship was working behind the scenes in all these incidents. I have no doubt that the vessel will make an appearance once more. Well, that last one, I might actually have to thank them for their help," Westcott said, shrugging playfully.

But the look on Ellen's face remained impassive as she replied, "You're certain about this? If we use *Goetia*, there's no holding back. I'm not entirely sure if it would stop with simply impeding them."

"Mm. I leave this matter to you," Westcott said. "Handle it as you please. If it does come to a crash, well, that will be the end for that ship."

Ellen nodded firmly.

School ended with Shido still missing. The sky, which had been so clear in the morning, was now cloudy, threatening rain at any moment. This plus the fact that the day was coming to an end meant that the area was already half-dark.

Tohka was walking down the road to the apartment building beside the Itsuka house, together with the Yamai sisters from the class next door.

"Hmph. This early departure of Shido's indicates weakness. He must train himself anew."

"Assent. Weak, wimpy weakling. Starting tomorrow, long training runs."

Tohka heard Kaguya first and then Yuzuru chiming in from behind her. She turned her head to look back and caught sight of the two girls with identical faces strolling alongside each other.

The girl on the right with the confident expression was Kaguya Yamai, while the one on the left with the sleepy look was Yuzuru Yamai. They were twin Spirits, impossible to tell apart at a glance, but any eyes that wandered slightly lower than the face would be able to see the extremely obvious difference between their bodies.

"Don't talk like that. I'm sure Shido has his reasons," Tohka said, and Kaguya and Yuzuru shrugged simultaneously.

"Kah-kah! We are aware. We joke. Well, it is perhaps true that I believe he could do with a little training."

"Question. That reminds me. I heard Master Origami transferred schools. Does Shido leaving early have something to do with that?" Yuzuru asked, angling her head to one side.

"Mm." Tohka furrowed her brow, troubled. "Shido *did* disappear right after he heard she transferred. Maybe there's a connection."

Kaguya and Yuzuru sniffed triumphantly.

"Keh-keh! Is that so? I smell something fishy."

"Assent. I do sniff a plot."

"Fishy?" Tohka looked up curiously. "It doesn't smell like fish, though?"

"No, that's not what it…" Kaguya scratched her cheek, sweat beading on her forehead. For some reason, she occasionally changed the way she spoke.

Before long, the Spirit apartment building where they lived came into view.

"Mm?" Tohka stopped in her tracks.

A girl was standing in front of Shido's house beside the apartment. Tall in a sailor-style uniform, bluish-purple hair fluttering in the breeze. Sensual, perfect proportions and a lovely face. But the expression on it was dark and brooding.

"Ah!"

The girl had apparently also noticed Tohka. Her dark expression brightened instantly, and she ran over, arms out in front of her.

"Tohkaaaaa! Kaguyaaaaaa! Yuzuruuuuu!"

"""…!"""

Tohka, Kaguya, and Yuzuru all leaped back immediately, sensing danger. But the girl kept barreling toward them and ended up with her arms wrapped around a telephone pole.

"Hngh! Honestly! Why would you run from meeee?" she said, thrusting her lips forward in a pout, still hanging onto the pole like a koala holding fast to a tree.

Her voice was beautiful, clear as a bell. And of course it was. She was a student at Rindoji Girls' Academy, but at the same time, she was one of Japan's top idols, Miku Izayoi.

"Well, why are you coming at us?!" Tohka half shouted the question.

"What? To hug you, oooobviously! It's an expression of loooove," Miku replied, as if it were the most natural thing in the world.

"I-it is…?" Tohka faltered.

"Yeees! Everyone does it. Come on, Tohka. You too!" Miku peeled herself away from the telephone pole and spread her arms out at Tohka.

Her proud pose made Tohka somehow start to feel like Miku was actually right.

"M-mm…"

That was when she found herself grabbed from behind, hands clamped tightly onto her shoulders.

"D-do not be fooled, my retainer!"

"Warning. I smell a lie."

The twins spoke from either side of her.

"...! I—I *knew* it!" Tohka gasped.

Miku's eyebrows pulled up into a sad semicircle. "Ohhh, come ooon. Don't worry. I promise to give you both warm hugs, too!"

"I never made such a request!"

"Shiver. I sense a danger to my person."

Kaguya and Yuzuru both stepped back, clutching their own shoulders now. Seeing this, Miku laughed out loud.

"Mm. Anyway, Miku, what are you doing here?" Tohka asked, and Miku blinked a few times before clapping her hands together as if just remembering the reason.

"Right, yes! School's over, so I came to be with my daaaarling, but no one's home. I stopped by the apartments next door, but you were all ouuuut. I've been so bored," she said petulantly.

Tohka and the Yamai sisters glanced at one another.

"Hmm?" Miku frowned. "What's the maaaatter?"

"Oh, uh," Tohka stammered, "Shido's still not home?"

"Nope! I rang the bell a few times, but there was nooo answer. Seems like Kotori's not home, either."

"Hmph. Perhaps this truly is connected with the incident with Origami."

"Assent. Something might be happening."

The Yamai sisters pressed their hands to their chins.

"Honestly!" Miku pursed her lips sulkily again. "Don't keep secrets! What on earth happened?"

"Mm. Hmm. The truth is..." Tohka summed up the situation briefly. Before her eyes, Miku began to radiate urgency and overwhelming curiosity.

"Hmmm, that is quite suspicious, iiisn't it?" she said. "My darling might be facing some kind of crisis."

"C-crisis? What do you mean?" Tohka started to sweat at the ominous word, and Miku held up a finger as she continued.

"Please take a moment to think about it. First, we can safely assume that Darling left early to go after Origami. And the fact that he still hasn't come home at this hour means..."

"…? Doesn't that just mean he hasn't found Origami Tobiichi yet?" Tohka asked.

Miku shook her head from side to side. "If that were the case, he would have called, at least. Which means…it's possible that he was caught by Origami and is being licked all oooover right this second!"

""""Wha…?!"""""

Tohka, Kaguya, and Yuzuru gaped at Miku. Was it possible that Shido, at that very moment…? Considering Origami's usual behavior, however, they couldn't reject this possibility out of hand. All three girls felt a shiver run up their spines.

"We caaaaan't simply stand here! We have to go look for him right now!" Miku said, and thrust an energetic fist into the air.

Tohka and the Yamai sisters followed suit, punching the air and crying out, """"Yeah!"""""

However.

Vwnnnnnnnnnnnnnnnnnnnnnnnnnnnmmmmm.

A shrill alarm began to blare.

"Mm. That's…" Tohka looked up.

"The…spacequake alarm," Miku murmured with a sour look.

But that only made sense. The alarm ringing meant that they would have to call off the search for Shido.

Just as the name suggested, a spacequake was a quaking of space. The cause of these unpredictable disasters was deemed to be the appearance of Spirits like Tohka.

"Ha! To wit, the appearance of a new Spirit?"

"Interest. I'm curious what kind of Spirit she is."

The Yamai sisters stroked their chins with deep curiosity. But Miku shook her head vigorously as if to admonish them.

"Oh, no, you don't," she said. "When the spacequake alarm goes off, we have to evacuate to a shelter."

"Mm. W-we are aware. It was merely a thought."

"Misfortune. We do not have a choice. Let's evacuate."

Kaguya and Yuzuru agreed reluctantly, and they started out for the neighborhood shelter.

"Mmm. But Shido…" Tohka, however, was frowning, troubled.

When the alarm sounded, they had to evacuate. She knew that. But what if Shido was in trouble out there? If they waited until the spacequake was over, Origami might have licked him down to nothing. Stuck on the idea, Tohka remained fixed to the spot.

"No need to evacuate," said a quiet voice from behind.

"Hmm…?" Tohka looked back suspiciously, and then her eyes grew wide.

Standing there was the very Origami Tobiichi whose transfer they had been informed of that morning.

"Origami Tobiichi…?" she said. "Why are you here?"

"Oh-ho? To think you would show yourself to us. You gleaned that it was futile attempting to run and hide from these evil eyes?"

"Admiration. Master Origami. Is it true about the school transfer?"

"Ohhh, Origami. Daaarling isn't with you?"

"…"

Origami didn't reply to any of the Spirits. She simply glared at the four of them quietly with eyes like ice.

Furrowing her brow at this, Tohka opened her mouth once more. "And what do you mean there's no need to evacuate?"

"There won't be a spacequake," Origami replied coolly.

"What?" Tohka tilted her head to one side, confused. "Isn't this the warning for a spacequake? Everyone's evacuating."

She waved a hand to indicate the residents in the area hurrying out of their houses and heading for the nearest shelter.

But Origami only stared wordlessly at Tohka and the other Spirits, almost like she was waiting for the residents to finish evacuating. Finally, she opened her mouth.

"This alarm is ringing at my request. There's no Spirit, no AST."

"What…?" Tohka asked. "Why on earth would you—?"

Origami looked at each of the Spirits' faces in turn again and took a deep breath as if to calm herself. Then she pulled what looked like a dog tag out of her pocket and touched it to her forehead lightly.

"So that I can kill you all here," she said.

She flashed with a pale light, and a Wizard's armor—a CR unit—appeared on her body. It was a dark gray and all sharp angles. The boosters deployed in a X shape, with a massive weapon equipped at the waist. This was not the usual official AST gear Origami normally wore. While the nature of the weapon was different, this unit looked very much like the equipment of DEM Industries Wizard Ellen Mathers.

"Wha—?!" Tohka cried out, stunned.

But Origami paid this no mind. She held out a hand in front of her, and the weapon equipped at her waist changed shape, deployed, and lodged itself in Origami's hand.

A huge magic gun, about as long as Origami was tall. The second it was at the ready, Origami pulled the trigger. A dazzling light flashed deep in the barrel, and an intense stream of magic shot out at the Spirits.

"Hngh!" Tohka immediately grabbed Miku and leaped to one side.

At the exact same moment, the Yamai sisters kicked at the ground and jumped up into the air.

In the next instant, a crater appeared in the place where the Spirits had only just been standing. The asphalt, the concrete wall alongside the road, all of it ripped up in a straight line leading back to Origami.

If they had retreated even a second slower, the Spirits would have been destroyed just like that wall.

Tohka glanced at the ends of her hair, scorched in the attack, and then glared at Origami.

"Wh-where'd that come from?!" she yelled. "You could've hurt someone!"

"I told you. I'm going to defeat you Spirits," Origami said in a cold voice as she turned the barrel of her weapon toward Tohka and Miku. There was no sign of any uncertainty or hesitation in her eyes.

This was not the usual Origami. Her gaze was pure hostility and bloodlust, and Tohka unconsciously swallowed hard at the anomaly.

"…!"

Tohka gritted her teeth. On second thought, she *had* seen this Origami before.

Over six months earlier, before Tohka met Shido, Origami and the AST had attacked Tohka every time she appeared in this world, and *that* Origami had looked at her in the same way as this one. The girl would risk her own life to hate the Spirits, despise the Spirits, kill the Spirits. The Origami before her now was precisely that Origami.

Because Tohka saw her all the time at school, she hadn't realized it until now, but Origami had obviously changed over the course of the past six months. Naturally, Shido's presence had a large hand in that, but the hatred she wielded against Tohka and the Yamai sisters had quietly and steadily turned into something different from what it had first been.

However, now.

"Why? Why did you go back, Origami Tobiichi?!" Tohka shouted.

"…"

Origami ignored her. Without a word, she got ready to pull the trigger again.

"Ngh…!" Tohka tried to leap up once again with Miku in her arms, but she was too late. A heartbeat before she could move, Origami's finger did.

But in that moment, the barrel was abruptly turned upward.

Tohka soon saw the reason for that. After fleeing the last shot up into the sky, the Yamai sisters had manifested limited Astral Dresses and were attacking Origami from above.

The beam of concentrated magic shot off into the clouds. But the Yamai sisters twisted around in the air and narrowly managed to avoid it.

"Keh-keh! Impressive instincts!"

"Respect. I would expect nothing less, Master Origami."

Kaguya and Yuzuru did a somersault in the air before dropping down to stand in front of Origami, as if to protect Tohka and Miku. And then they struck cool poses as they turned the Angels in their hands on Origami.

"Now then, shall we hear a word of explanation from you, Origami? Is this not somewhat excessive as a jest?"

"Interrogation. Please answer her, Master Origami. I have no wish to fight with you."

"I don't have to answer you."

The words were no sooner out of her mouth than Origami was manipulating the magic gun to make an enormous blade appear at the end of it, wrapped in magic. She held up the laser blade and charged the Yamai sisters. She had most likely popped up a Territory around herself; she accelerated suddenly with no advance warning. A normal opponent would have been cut down without even the chance to counter the movement.

But the Yamai sisters boasted the greatest agility of all the Spirits. They dodged the blow and launched their own offensive against Origami.

However, the battle was definitely not in their favor. Origami had probably expanded her Territory to hinder their movement. They were being gradually pushed back.

"Ngh!" Tohka groaned. "Miku, we have to help them!"

"R-right!"

The Yamai sisters were in trouble. The moment Tohka had this thought, light enveloped her body and took shape as her Astral Dress.

"Sandalphon!" she cried, and thrust her right hand out. Particles of light began gathering to manifest her Angel, Sandalphon. This was the most powerful sword, able to slice through anything in its path.

At the same time, a number of silver pipes appeared around Origami, and the sound of an instrument began to ring out in the area. It was Miku. Having manifested a limited version of her Angel, Gabriel, like Tohka and the Yamai sisters, she was playing a keyboard of light to produce an elegant melody.

"Gabriel. Rondo!"

"…!"

Origami furrowed her brow just a hint. The sound that came out of Miku's Angel, Gabriel, bound Origami's body.

Miku didn't want to kill Origami. But as things stood, they couldn't have a real conversation unless something changed.

Tohka exchanged a look with the Yamai sisters dancing in the sky, and they flew at Origami at the same time from three different directions.

"Aaaaaaah!" Tohka brandished Sandalphon and brought it down on Origami. At the same time, Kaguya's lance closed in from the right, and Yuzuru's pendulum from the left.

There was nowhere for her to go. The Spirits' timing was impeccable. Even clad in DEM equipment, Origami wouldn't escape unscathed after a simultaneous Angel attack.

However.

"Haah!"

"…?!"

Origami let out a fierce battle cry, and the silver cylinders around her were knocked away. At the same time, Tohka felt an invisible hand grab hold of her.

"Wha…?!" She knew this sensation. It was astoundingly similar to the time she'd been held prisoner by Ellen Mathers and her super-concentrated Territory. It felt like she'd been plunged into a quagmire; her limbs no longer moved freely, and even breathing was difficult.

It didn't last long, however. Three seconds at most. However, that brief pause was enough to change the balance of power.

"…!"

Origami imbued her laser blade with magic and made it flash.

"Hngh!"

"Gah!"

"Sorrow. Ungh!"

Although Tohka just barely managed to catch the blow with her sword, she couldn't absorb the full impact. She and the Yamai sisters let out cries of anguish and were knocked flying in different directions.

"Cough! Cough!"

"I-is everyone okaaay?!"

Tohka heard Miku's worried voice from behind. But she couldn't respond to it. The reason was simple. Having knocked Tohka and the twins flying, Origami was still on them, a sharp gleam in her eyes as she glared at them.

Tohka was quite certain that if she looked away for even an instant, her head would be dancing up into the air.

Origami was seriously out for blood.

The reality of what Origami had said earlier finally sank into her bones.

Origami was trying to kill them, and she actually had the power to make that happen.

Knock her unconscious and finish this? Fight but don't kill her and try to talk? Though only a few scant minutes had passed, Tohka realized now how naive those thoughts had been.

The person standing before them was a powerful, hostile opponent with deadly intentions and the strength to match.

It was kill or be killed. That was the unspoken rule of the battlefield she thought she'd left behind six months ago. She felt ice engulf her heart.

"...!"

She gulped hard. Even with this dawning on her, she couldn't find it in herself to kill Origami.

It wasn't just Origami who had changed these past months. Tohka realized finally that as they spent time together, the hatred and hostility she had felt toward the other girl had turned into something else.

"What are you doing, Tohka?!"

"...?!"

She jerked her head up at Kaguya's abrupt cry. In the fleeting instant that she'd let her thoughts wander, Origami had started to charge her and was now closing in fast before her eyes.

"Hwah!"

"Ngh! Ah!"

The blow that hit her was merciless. Her supposedly absolute Astral Dress was ripped apart, and blood scattered all around her.

"The spacequake alarm?! Is there a Spirit signal in the area?" Kotori cried out, crimson jacket hanging over her shoulders as she sat on the bridge of the airship *Fraxinus*, fifteen thousand meters in the air above the city of Tengu.

They had been searching for the still-missing Shido when the space-quake alarm abruptly sounded in Tengu.

"N-no Spirit signal detected!" Minowa called out as she tapped at a device on the lower level of the bridge.

Kotori furrowed her brow at this entirely expected response. Given that *Fraxinus* was equipped with the world's best Spirit measurement equipment, there was no way the ship would have missed picking up the signal before the SDF did. In which case, this was...

"A false alarm?" she asked.

"...No, it might be dangerous to assume that," a woman said, a sleepy look on her face and noticeably dark bags under her eyes. She was a Ratatoskr analyst and Kotori's good friend, Reine Murasame.

"Meaning?"

"...Think about it. When Shin broke into DEM's Japanese office two months ago, the spacequake alarm sounded then, too."

Kotori's eyebrows arched up. It was true that DEM or someone in the higher echelons of the SDF could set off the alarm.

"Then is this just to clear people out?" she asked. "They're about to do something that requires the residents of the area to evacuate?"

"...It's quite possible. At the very least, it's dangerous to assume that it's a simple false alarm."

It was indeed exactly as Reine said. Kotori flicked up the stick of the Chupa Chups in her mouth and called to the lower level of the bridge, "Investigate the situation within the alarm area immediately. Take some of the autonomous cameras and drones we've got on the search for Shido and—"

A shrill ringing on the bridge interrupted her.

"...! What is it?!" she called.

"Sir! Confirmation of a powerful magic signal in the vicinity of your house, Commander! Tohka and the other Spirits are there, too!"

"What did you say? Put it on-screen," she snapped. "Now!"

"Yes, sir!"

As the crew member tapped at their console, a familiar neighborhood appeared on the main monitor on the bridge.

"Wha—?!" Kotori gasped, a shiver running up her spine.

That was the only natural response because whatever else was happening, Tohka, the Yamai sisters, and Miku were facing off against Origami Tobiichi clad in a DEM CR unit in front of the Itsuka house.

"Origami Tobiichi...?! What is she doing there?!"

It was obvious that the girls were not merely having a pleasant chat. In fact, only seconds after Kotori cried out, Origami began to attack the Spirits.

"Ngh!" she groaned.

"Th-these magic values are incredible!" Kawagoe half shrieked from the lower deck. "Her numbers from before don't even begin to compare! And with Tohka and the other Spirits only in limited Astral Dresses...!"

Kotori screwed up her face in annoyance. She didn't know what had happened between DEM and Origami. But it was clear that the Spirits were in danger. She raised a hand and called out to her crew.

"*Fraxinus*, full speed ahead! We're picking up Tohka and the others! If we hit trouble, deploy Yggdrafolium for backup!"

"Roger!" her crew responded in unison, and the faint sound of motors on the bridge grew louder.

Fraxinus changed course for Kotori's house—only to be stopped by a fierce shock.

"...?!" Kotori gasped. "What's happening?!"

"An external attack! Territory's down thirty percent!"

"…! Enemy sighting at our three o'clock! It's…an airship!"

"What did you say?!" Kotori shouted as an enormous ship appeared on the main monitor.

To be more precise, empty space twisted, and an airship appeared in it. There should have been no way that such a massive lump of steel could materialize that abruptly. It must have had Invisible deployed the way *Fraxinus* had.

"That's…" Kotori was at a loss for words when she saw the ship on-screen.

It was a streamlined machine, more or less the same size as *Fraxinus*, boasting beautiful platinum armor decorated with lavish gold detailing.

Since there were only two companies in the world that could produce Realizers, this was most likely a DEM ship. But it made an entirely different impression from the two DEM ships Kotori and her crew had seen thus far. If those ships had been weapons for battle, this ship before *Fraxinus* now was built for pomp and ceremony, to ferry nobility.

But Kotori shook her head to clear that thought away.

Given that the massive bulk of the airship was held aloft by the permanent Territory generated by Realizers, the crafts still could not be openly listed in the public record. However much its decorations made it seem like a horse carriage of old, it couldn't be shown off anywhere, and more importantly, no matter how capricious DEM might have been, they wouldn't bring a ship designed with nothing more than a "look at me" attitude to attack *Fraxinus*.

Regardless of how out of place it seemed, the thing floating before her eyes was intended as a special agent of destruction dispatched by DEM Industries.

"Tch! At a time like this!" Kotori gritted her teeth until they squealed.

Actually, maybe it was precisely *because* it was a time like this. It was hard to imagine that there was no connection between Origami's belligerent entrance and this airship. Most likely, they'd assumed that

Kotori would set off to help the Spirits and prepared a net in the sky to prevent that.

They could manipulate their Territory and use the optical camouflage Invisible to cause the ship to blend into the sky around them, but this function was only fully effective when the ship was stationary. If it began to move with the camouflage deployed, distortions in the surrounding area could be seen, albeit very slight ones.

As Kotori clenched her jaw in vexation, an alarm began to blare over the speakers.

"What now?!" she cried, and Shiizaki on the lower bridge tapped at her console, gasping in surprise.

"It's…an incoming call! The ship is pinging Fraxinus's frequency!"

"A call…?" Kotori furrowed her brow doubtfully. "Put it through."

"Yes, sir!"

A window opened on the monitor, and the figure of a young girl was displayed. Her blond hair and blue eyes suggested she was a Westerner. An absolute confidence in herself could be seen in her sharp features.

"*How do you do? I suppose this is our first meeting. I appreciate you responding to my call,*" the girl said in fluent Japanese.

Kotori almost gasped. "Ellen Mathers?!"

Yes. Shown on the screen was DEM Industries second enforcement division Wizard, Ellen M. Mathers.

"Wha…?!"

Kotori heard the crew on the lower deck all cry as one.

But this was only natural. Whatever else, the person on-screen was supposedly humanity's most powerful Wizard, with strength comparable to a Spirit but in a human body, and she'd been specially noted as a subject requiring the utmost caution.

Ellen arched an eyebrow. "*Do you know of me? I'm honored. Kotori Itsuka.*"

She spoke Kotori's name as if it was payback, likely trying to imply that she had also done her homework. In contrast with her elegant appearance, this was a woman who hated to lose.

Kotori sniffed derisively and glared at her.

"Yes. You got a problem with that? Maybe you think a junior high kid like me is just playing at commander?"

"Of course not. Individual ability has no connection with appearance or age. I must express my respect for your skill, seeing how you interfered with our previous activities; I wouldn't presume to offer any complaint," Ellen replied very solemnly.

Unable to see what Ellen's intentions were, Kotori narrowed her eyes slightly. "Well, thanks. So what does the world's most powerful Wizard want from us exactly? If it's an invitation to tea, could it wait? I'm a bit busy at the moment. It appears that a rogue employee of a corrupt corporation has come out to bother my girls," she said sarcastically, but the look on Ellen's face didn't change.

In a dispassionate tone, she responded to Kotori's question. *"I have two matters of business. One. I shall allow you three minutes. Those of you who value your lives, please leave the ship immediately."*

"What did you say...?" Kotori's gaze sharpened even further, and she snorted. "You're boldly claiming that you're planning to shoot down *Fraxinus*?"

"I cannot deny the possibility that this will be the end result. However, Fraxinus... Is that the name of the ship, then? I see. An effective play on 'world tree.' I suppose it was Elliot who named it?"

Kotori's eyes widened slightly at Elliot's name.

Elliot Baldwin Woodman, the founder of Ratatoskr and chairperson of the Ratatoskr decision-making body, Rounds.

But she had more important things to focus on right now. She let out an irritated sigh and glared at her enemy through the screen with a murderous gaze.

"Think you might be underestimating *Fraxinus* here," she said.

"With all due respect, perhaps you are the one who is miscalculating? Of the performance of Goetia. And of my power."

"..."

Kotori couldn't hear any hint of playfulness in Ellen's voice. She was seriously saying that her ship would beat *Fraxinus*, the airship that

was the crystallization of the best technologies Asgard Electronics had to offer.

"Hmph," she sniffed. "So then why bother to try and get rid of some of the crew, reduce our numbers? Sounds to me like you don't have a chance of winning, so you want to whittle down our strength with some fancy words."

"*That is connected to the second matter,*" Ellen said evenly. This was an adversary who could not be rattled.

Kotori clicked her tongue in annoyance. "Hmm? And what would that be?"

Ellen exhaled slowly and nodded deeply. "*Yes. I would like to ask those who flee this battle to convey a message to Elliot.*"

"A message?"

"*Yes,*" Ellen affirmed quietly, and for the first time, emotion colored her flat voice. "*Elliot. Elliot. You traitor. You double-crosser, turning your back on our promise! Get ready. No matter where you try to hide, I will find you and remove that head from your neck!*"

"…?!"

Kotori unconsciously gasped at the fiery words. This level of intensity seemed unthinkable coming from Ellen.

The blond girl cleared her throat, recomposed her expression, and turned her eyes on Kotori. "*That is the message. Now, I will wait for three minutes. Please go ahead and flee.*"

"You hear that?" Kotori looked out over her crew on the lower deck of the bridge and announced with a straight face, deadly serious, "Our enemy is one of humanity's most powerful. If you want to run, I won't hold it against you."

Her crew flinched, but the corners of their mouths all turned up.

"Ridiculous," one said. "If I was going to run at a time like this, I would never have followed you in the first place, Commander."

"Agreed," called another. "How is leaving you here and running any different from death?"

"Right," a third chimed in. "I don't know about humanity's most powerful, but we can show her what we're made of."

"Orders, Commander. I already wrote up my will long ago."

"I-I've also set it up so that the data on the D drive on my home computer will be erased if I die!"

The crew spoke one after another. And then Kannazuki, standing behind the captain's chair, nodded firmly.

"Of course I'll stay," he declared. "Although, it *is* hard to pass up the opportunity to flee and be thoroughly punished by you, Commander."

"..."

Without a word, Kotori stomped on Kannazuki's foot.

"Eeeek!" came an ecstatic cry from behind her.

Kotori sighed and turned back to the screen. "There you have it."

"*Is that so? How unfortunate,*" Ellen said, the look on her face indeed one of regret.

Kotori waved a hand and let fly with orders to the lower deck. "Parallel operation of AR-008 numbers three through six! Begin magic charging. Ready Mistilteinn! Target on our three o'clock! DEM airship *Goetia*!"

"Roger!"

As if spurred into action by Kotori's voice, the crew began to punch commands into their consoles as one.

Seeing this reaction, Ellen narrowed her eyes slightly and leaned back in her chair. Actually, it was shaped somewhat differently from a chair—more like a hyperbaric chamber set at an angle. It strangely resembled a metal coffin or a sleeping pod from a science fiction film.

There was also what appeared to be a headset at the top of the coffin/chair. Kotori had seen a device like this before. It was a unit to substitute a human brain for the airship's control Realizer. Although the look was different, there was similar equipment installed on *Fraxinus*.

"*Kotori Itsuka. I had thought you would be able to make decisions with a cooler head. But you truly are the sister of Shido Itsuka even if you are not related by blood, hmm?*"

"The highest compliment," Kotori said with a derisive sniff before tapping at her personal console to end the transmission. "Active Yggdrafolium, one through twelve! Kannazuki!"

"Sir!" Kyohei Kannazuki, the vice commander of *Fraxinus*, responded from his position next to the captain's seat.

"We're up against the world's most powerful Wizard," she said. "Be ready, just in case."

"I thought you might say that," Kannazuki said in return. Kotori glanced back and saw him standing there with a headset on already.

The corners of her mouth turned up, and she pinched the stick of the Chupa Chups in her mouth between her fingers and popped the lollipop out of her mouth.

"We can't stick around and play with her all day!" she shouted. "Let's finish this up quick and hurry to the Spirits!"

"Yes, sir!"

"Magic charging complete. Mistilteinn is ready to fire at any time!"

"No movement from the enemy ship *Goetia*!"

Kotori clicked her tongue. It was unbelievable that Ellen wasn't taking any action despite the fact that the battle had started. Negotiations had broken down, and their opponent wasn't so happy-go-lucky as to politely wait out the declared three minutes. Assuming Ellen wasn't a total dunce, this had to mean she intended to cede the first strike to them.

In which case, she was severely underestimating *Fraxinus*. Kotori snapped her Chupa Chups at the enemy ship on-screen.

"Mistilteinn, fire!" she cried, her voice ringing out across the bridge, and dazzling light jetted from the guns on the airship's bow.

This vast quantity of magic was generated by the daisy-chained Realizers the ship carried for battle. A devastating light that turned everything it touched to dust blasted through the air. Their timing was perfect. Ellen wouldn't be able to completely dodge the shot with the sluggish movement of a bulky airship.

Naturally, given that their enemy also had a Territory deployed, Kotori wasn't foolish enough to assume that this would be a decisive blow. The way Ellen's ship simply floated in the air without moving, as if issuing a challenge, must have meant she had quite a lot of faith in her Territory.

But creating a starting point for the attack and seizing the initiative were critical in a battle between airships. All the magic was worth it if it meant they could whittle away at their opponent's Territory. And if they could make their opponent concentrate their defensive Territory in the front of the airship to avoid *Fraxinus*'s guns, then they also had the option of turning the Yggdrafolium they'd already released into the air into mines and detonating them at the enemy's rear.

Either way, starting now, they'd focus purely on attacking. If Ellen really wanted to knock *Fraxinus* out of the sky, then her only shot would have been to not contact them at all and launch an assault immediately after her initial surprise appearance.

However.

"Wha…?!" Kotori's eyes flew open in surprise.

Just as Mistilteinn's light was about to touch it, *Goetia* shifted to the left unbelievably fast and dodged the blast by a hair.

It was a normally unthinkable move. The ship had not advanced or retreated or turned; it simply went straight off to the side. An incredibly unnatural movement, almost like a pawn on a chessboard sliding to the adjacent square.

"What was that…?!" she cried.

"Hmm," Kannazuki said, stroking his chin. "It appears that she made the Territory enveloping the ship as thin as possible for increased maneuverability. She then most likely slingshotted the ship with the Territory."

"Is something like that even possible?!"

"In theory, it's not *im*possible, although I've never tried it. I suppose this is what we can expect from the Eternal Mathers."

Kotori slammed a hand down on the armrest of her captain's chair. "This is no time to admire her moves! Here she comes!"

At the same time as she shouted, *Goetia* charged toward *Fraxinus* in yet another unnatural trajectory, far too fast for an airship.

"Ngh!" she groaned. "Territory to defensive! Brace for impact!"

"Yes, sir!"

No sooner had the gun on *Goetia*'s prow fired than the blast was slamming into the Territory enveloping *Fraxinus*, sending magic light arcing like bolts of electricity.

"Tch! So she wants to play. Set Yggdrafolium to mine mode! Hit *Goetia* in the rear!" Kotori barked orders to the lower deck of the bridge. They had to launch a counterattack before she was able to fire again.

As the name suggested, Yggdrafolium was a group of leaf-shaped units equipped on *Fraxinus*. Each had an independent Realizer and was able to deploy a Territory through remote operation by the mother ship. As general weaponry, they had a truly wide variety of applications from interrupting communications to attacking the enemy. The presence of this unique weapon was also the biggest feature of the Asgard Electronics–made airship *Fraxinus*.

"Roge— Ah!"

However. Something anomalous occurred. Just as the crew started to call out in response to Kotori, a shrill alarm rang out on the bridge.

"What is it?!" their commander yelled.

"It's… She's firing again!"

"What did you…?!" Kotori gasped as *Goetia*'s nose flashed, and the bridge of Fraxinus rocked violently back and forth.

"Ngh!" Gritting her teeth, Kotori glared at the enemy ship on-screen.

It went without saying that the main armament of an airship were the magic cannons and guns that shot magic missiles produced by the Realizers. Although they did have conventional weapons on board, they were almost entirely useless in a fight between airships shielded by Territories.

The key was to wear down the opponent's Territory. Excluding specialized weaponry like Yggdrafolium, the viable attack options were limited to a blast from a magic gun or increasing Territory strength and slamming directly into the opponent.

Thus, the strategy undertaken by *Goetia* was extremely orthodox. Except for the abnormal speed.

"Firing again before even ten seconds have passed since the initial shot?!" Kotori said. "Absurd! What kind of Realizer could…?!"

Given that the Realizers had to operate in parallel to generate magic, rapid fire from the main arms was, as a general principle, not possible. Even *Fraxinus* needed thirty seconds before their next shot, no matter how much they hurried.

It might have seemed like a simple matter of increasing the number of magic-generating Realizers to speed up the process. But it wasn't. With the increase in the amount of magic generated, there came limits in physical capacity. Unless the vehicle was operating at incredible efficiency...

"Tch!" Kotori clicked her tongue in annoyance. The abnormal movement of the ship. The rapid-fire magic gun. They were linked to the figure of Ellen Mathers she'd seen earlier.

Although the gap in Realizer performance itself had been closed with DEM's new Ashcroft-β units, Ratatoskr was still on top. Which was exactly why DEM had come up with a different approach to overcome the technology gap.

Rather than only having this option as an emergency measure as *Fraxinus* did, DEM added the processing abilities of the human brain right from step one for more efficient operation, making their vessel a pure warship. This type of foul technique was possible precisely because they had Ellen, an almost impossibly powerful Wizard.

Naturally, the burden on the brain was far greater than that of a normal CR unit. Most likely, continuous operation of the ship over a long period was impossible even for Ellen.

But in front of *Fraxinus* at that moment was not a sluggish airship requiring a crew of people to operate it; this was Ellen M. Mathers herself clad in a supersized CR unit.

"Commander!" one of Kotori's crew called out. "Portside Territory is reaching threshold values!"

"Tch!" She looked at her personal monitor and saw that, indeed, part of the Territory had been severely damaged.

"Redeploy Territory!" she barked. "And get Mistilteinn recharged already!"

"R-roger!" came the response.

"Kannazuki!" she snapped.

"Sir!" Guessing at her intention, Kannazuki's eyes grew sharper. Instantly, Yggdrafolium shot through the air at tremendous speed.

The *Fraxinus* control Realizer was not directing Yggdrafolium at that moment. The one holding the reins now was Kannazuki, the vice commander on standby behind the captain's chair.

Yggdrafolium danced through the air and moved to circle around *Goetia*. The Territory generated around the leaf-shaped weapons expanded outward, stretching in unison.

It was creating a cage in midair, enclosing the enemy airship.

"Commander, you're clear," Kannazuki said.

"Good. Mistilteinn...fire!" Kotori shouted, pointing her Chupa Chups at *Goetia*.

As if in response, the recharged, concentrated magic cannon Mistilteinn drew a line of light in the sky.

A magic missile from the front. If Ellen tried to evade it, the Yggdrafolium mines were waiting all around her. Even swift *Goetia* wouldn't be able to dodge this blow.

The instant Mistilteinn was fired, however, when it looked like this shot was headed straight for *Goetia*, the ship body angled to one side and dodged the magic bullet, grazing Yggdrafolium's Territory as it did.

"What did she...?!" Kotori gaped.

Naturally, upon detecting this impact, Yggdrafolium detonated to cause a terrific explosion, but *Goetia* was untouched. Ellen had most likely concentrated the Territory blanketing the ship to a point to defend against the explosion.

"Does this woman have nerves of steel?!" Kotori gritted her teeth in vexation.

That had been a risky maneuver. If Ellen's handling had been the tiniest bit off, she would have been smashed to smithereens. Any sane person would have specialized their defensive Territory in the direction of the beam of magic and tried to survive the blast.

In fact, the moment her opponent did just that, Kotori had been planning to order a follow-up attack with Yggdrafolium. In a game of escalating bluffs, Ellen was the clear winner. It was because she'd seen through Kotori's tactic that she'd risked such danger.

"Tch..." Kotori grimaced. She couldn't help but feel that the woman didn't think the maneuver had even been a risk at all. She felt like Ellen had simply evaded the attack as if it were the most natural thing in the world—based on her own arrogance, the conviction that it would have been impossible for her to *not* pull it off.

"*Goetia* is approaching!" Mikimoto half shrieked from the lower deck.

Having dodged Mistilteinn, *Goetia* was charging straight at *Fraxinus*.

"Ngh! Evasive—," Kotori started, but she was interrupted by Kannazuki.

"Please don't worry, Commander." Headset on, he stepped out from beside the captain's seat and snapped his fingers.

Instantly, the Mistilteinn beam, which *Goetia* had dodged, took a sharp turn behind the enemy airship and turned right around.

"Ah!" For a moment, Kotori didn't understand what had happened, but she quickly caught on.

Countless Yggdrafolium were floating to the rear of *Goetia* with Territories deployed. Kannazuki had manipulated these fields to forcibly twist the trajectory of the magic attack.

This was indeed unexpected, apparently. Mistilteinn ripped into the defenseless stern of *Goetia* and exploded.

Yes. If Ellen was a monster, well, *Fraxinus* had a monster, too. Kotori looked up at the tall man standing next to her chair and exhaled.

"Wouldn't expect anything less, Kannazuki."

"Much obliged." He bowed neatly. "I couldn't exactly allow our beautiful world tree to be injured. And..."

"And?" Kotori prodded when he hesitated.

"...I think you are much more wonderful, Commander, when you are doing the attacking rather than the one being attacked!" he shouted, clenching his hands into fists.

Kotori sighed.

"...! Commander! *Goetia*'s—!" Nakatsugawa screamed, and Kotori's shoulders jumped up.

Goetia was supposed to have been hit by Mistilteinn, and yet it was clearly charging at top speed toward *Fraxinus*.

"Wha…?!"

Goetia focused its magic and fired.

The main monitor on the bridge of *Fraxinus* was filled with a dazzling light.

Chapter 3
Angel

Going back in time an hour or so.

Shido writhed desperately in the chair he was tied to in an abandoned building.

"Ngh! Come off!" he cried.

There was no way, however, that banging his arms into the chair was going to remove the metal handcuffs. Similarly, the chair was bolted to the floor and didn't so much as budge.

"Dammit! I don't have time for this! Origami! Origamiiii!" he shouted, but no one appeared in response. He heard his own voice echo emptily off the walls and grimaced.

He had no idea what part of town he was in, but it seemed like there was absolutely no one around. About all he could hear was the squealing of the door battered by the wind and the occasional car honking off in the distance.

Still, that was perhaps only natural. Origami had carefully selected and prepared this location for the express purpose of confining him. It wouldn't have been some place anyone could accidentally stumble upon.

But…he couldn't quite resign himself to despair just yet.

After spending this much time with her, he had come to understand her way of thinking. He was pretty sure she wouldn't have chosen to lock him up in a place where absolutely no one came by.

His reasoning was simple. In the case where Origami was the only person who knew about this location, then if something happened to her, there would be no one to save Shido.

Naturally, it was also possible that she had set up a program to e-mail the school or the police after a certain amount of time had passed, but as the bare minimum insurance, he felt like Origami would have put some consideration into seeing that someone came by every couple of days—just enough time to make sure Shido didn't starve to death.

In this case in particular, Origami's objective was to keep him from getting caught up in her fight with the Spirits. If she could keep Shido nailed down here today, then that would stop being an issue.

In which case, someone meaning to come by every couple of days might feel a little capricious. Betting on this small chance, Shido kept yelling:

"Someone! Is anyone out there?!"

All he could do was have faith in Origami. Ignoring the pain in his throat, he shouted as loudly as he could.

But no matter how much he yelled, all he heard in response was the echo of his own voice.

"Ngh…"

If only he could call someone. But of course, Origami had taken his phone. Once they realized Shido was missing, Kotori and Ratatoskr would start looking for him, but that would be too late.

"Dammit. What am I supposed to do here?!" Knowing it was useless, Shido threw himself around in the chair.

Then.

"Huh…?" His eyes flew open wide. He was sure he'd heard something other than the creaking of the chair. He stopped moving and perked his ears. Before too long, he realized the sound was teensy tiny footsteps coming from the other side of the door before him.

"…! I-is someone there?!" he called loudly. Divine intervention. There was no way he was letting this chance slip away.

As if the footsteps had heard this cry, they slowly approached and stopped in front of the door to the room where he was being held.

However.

When he saw who opened the door, making the rusty hinges squeal, his face, which had started to relax in relief, tensed up once more.

"O-Origami…?!"

Yes. Standing there was the very person who had tied Shido up here. It was Origami Tobiichi.

"…"

She walked over to Shido silently.

He was momentarily shocked, but then he quickly shook his head as if to get his thoughts back on track.

"Origami, you came back for me?" he asked.

"…"

She still said nothing. Moving forward at the same pace, she came to stand in front of him.

"Origami…?" He frowned at the silent girl. "You're—"

He gasped at the possibility that abruptly flashed through his mind.

At first, he thought that Origami might've had a change of heart and come back to him. A selfish assumption. When he thought about it with a more level head, he understood only too well how soft and hopefully optimistic this was.

Origami Tobiichi's will and self-control were stronger than those of anyone else he'd ever known. It was impossible she would have changed her mind for no reason whatsoever.

In which case, why *had* she come back?

He could think of only two reasons. One was that some kind of issue had come up, forcing her to return to Shido. And the other, because she had already achieved her objective.

"…!" Shido swallowed hard and looked into her eyes. "Origami, why…did you come back?"

"…"

She did not respond but simply returned his gaze silently.

He started breathing faster at the mechanical expression on her face, devoid of all emotion. His heart pounded faster, and his throat grew absurdly dry.

"Y-you didn't actually...," he said, his voice trembling, and Origami reacted at last.

But it was neither a confirmation nor a denial. The corners of her mouth slid upward to form a smile.

"Wha...?" He felt his heart constrict at this expression.

And of course he did. Whatever else, it was Origami Tobiichi standing before him. The look on her face rarely changed, if ever. With the features to match the lack of expression, she could truly be described as doll-like. Even on those rare occasions when she did frown or relax her cheeks, he had never seen her produce anything so clearly labeled a smile as this.

Maybe this was why he hadn't been able to read any emotion in her face the time he first saw her.

"Wh-why are you...smiling, Origami...?" he asked, and her smile grew even wider. Her body began to shake as if she couldn't hold it in any longer.

"Pft! Heh-heh! Heh-heh-heh!"

And the laughter steadily grew louder.

"Heh-heh! Ah-ha-ha! Ha-ha... Ha-ha-ha-ha-ha-ha-ha-ha-ha-ha-ha-ha-ha!"

Origami doubled over in laughter.

"O...ri...ga...mi?" Shido could only gape at this abnormal sight.

He had no idea what this laughter meant. But he was at least painfully aware of the fact that this was not the usual Origami before him. His heart was hammering in his chest.

But he soon noticed something was off. He felt like the laughing was a little over-the-top.

"Hee-hee-hee! Your face! The look on your face! Ah-ha-ha-ha-ha! It's so funny! So weird! Aah, I can't breathe!"

"...Origami?" Shido said with a frown, a drop of sweat rolling down his cheek.

Origami was rolling around on the floor, clutching her stomach. She was flailing so hard that from time to time, he caught a glimpse of her panties under her skirt. They were white.

While she was cracking up, the door she had come in through opened once more, and another girl stepped inside.

She was a small girl in a cute newsboy cap, with a rabbit puppet on her left hand. When he saw her, Shido cried out automatically.

"Yoshino?!"

"Y-yes… Are you all right, Shido?" she said, a concerned look on her face. As if to go along with this, Yoshinon flapped its mouth.

"Aaah, this is one heck of an abduction. Hey, Yoshino, this is your chance. You can do whatever you want to Shido right now!"

"…!"

Yoshino's cheeks flushed bright red, and she put a hand over Yoshinon's mouth.

Although he wasn't unconcerned about Yoshinon's ominous statement, now was not the time for that.

"Run, Yoshino!" he cried out. "Origami's not her usual self here!"

He didn't know what Yoshino was doing there. But he could easily see just how dangerous it was for her to be exposed to Origami after the older girl had declared she was going to kill the Spirits before she left him there.

But Yoshino merely blinked her large eyes several times and then looked at Origami still rolling around on the floor laughing.

And then with no fear, she opened her mouth quietly. "Umm… I think that's enough now…?"

"Heh. Heh-heh… Hee-hee… Hee…"

Origami finally settled down and stood up. She pushed back her tangled bangs, a daring smile creeping across her face as she emitted a faint light.

"Wha—?" Shido stared, eyes wide, as the silhouette of Origami gradually grew smaller—and turned into a girl he knew. "Natsumi?!"

Yes. Appearing before him was the Spirit who had woken him up that morning, Natsumi, in her true form. She had transformed into Origami. No wonder Origami had been acting so strangely.

He let out a sigh of relief at the fact that this Origami was a fake and that the two Spirits were okay.

But perhaps Natsumi took that sigh in a different way. She looked toward him with a frown. "What? You got a problem? You're not happy I'm here?"

"Oh, uh, it's not that. But what *are* you two doing here?" he asked, and Yoshino and Natsumi exchanged a glance.

"Um," Yoshino said, "I was showing…Natsumi around town…"

"And we saw you walking off somewhere with Origami for some reason." Natsumi continued. "Yoshino had to know what was up, so we followed—"

"N-Natsumi…" Yoshino tugged on Natsumi's sleeve, looking embarrassed.

"Ah!" Natsumi also turned red and grabbed Yoshino's shirttail. The bashful pair clutched at each other's clothes. It was an odd sight.

"A-anyway! I'm glad you're here! Can you get me out of this rope and these handcuffs?" he asked, and the girls looked at each other again.

They nodded firmly and went around behind him to start picking at the handcuffs and pulling at the knots. But.

"Sh-Shido," Yoshino said. "Is there a…key for these handcuffs?"

"Whoa, what's with this rope?" Natsumi complained. "The knots are super complicated. And they're glued together…"

Apparently, he had underestimated Origami. It was great that help had arrived, but he was still stuck.

But then Natsumi thumped her own chest. "Welp. I guess I'll have to handle this."

"Huh?" Shido asked. "What are you going to do?"

"Just wait and see," Natsumi replied, closed her eyes, and stood silently for a moment.

A few seconds later, her face scrunched up from what seemed to be pain, her fingers moved to scratch at her throat, and then her eyes abruptly flew open.

"Shut your big fat mouths!" she screamed incomprehensibly.

In that instant, Shido's bindings shone faintly and turned into fluffy cotton.

"Th-this…!" He stared in surprise as he brought his hands around to the front of his body. "Natsumi, this Spirit power, how are you…?"

Natsumi let out an exhausted sigh as she wiped the sweat from her forehead. "Mm. I noticed that when I feel bad, a bit of my power comes back to me, y'know? So I kinda had an idea I could manage something at least."

"When you think about feeling bad?" Shido asked.

"Yeah." She nodded. "Just now, I imagined something like, I'm eating lunch by myself in a toilet stall at school because I don't have any friends, but I forgot to lock the door, and someone from my class opens it."

"Whoa," he said. "That *would* be embarrassing."

"And then when I get back to class," she said, continuing, "I sorta get the feeling that everyone's looking at me and laughing. They're all whispering stuff like 'Huh? For real? So that actually happens? Whoa, isn't that totally deadly?'"

"Stop! We get it!" The scene was so cringe-inducing that Shido unconsciously covered his ears.

But he quickly realized that he had more important things to deal with at the moment. He pulled away the cotton wrapped around him and stood up from the chair. Because he'd been stuck in the same position for such a long time, his joints ached.

They had to hurry back to Tohka and the other Spirits. In the worst-case scenario, Origami might have already made contact with them.

"Ah!" he said. "Right…! Do either of you have a phone I can borrow?"

"Huh? Oh, yes. Here." Yoshino pulled a blue phone out of her pocket.

He accepted this with a "thank you," selected ITSUKA HOUSE (2) in the address book, and placed the call.

This ITSUKA HOUSE (2) was code for *Fraxinus*. This number had been registered in the phones given to all the Spirits without exception so that they could call in case of an emergency.

If he could just get in touch with the airship, they could use the transporter device and dash over to Tohka and the others right away. At worst, he would at least be able to ask Kotori to back up the Spirits.

But instead of a ringing or the voice of one of the crew, all he heard from the earpiece of the phone was a mechanical buzzing.

"What's going on?" He frowned at the phone in his hand.

It would have been a different story if he'd been calling Kotori's personal number, but this was the general line to *Fraxinus*. He remembered Kotori telling him that they used a landline to allow for transmission even in the event that cell phone towers were blown away in a spacequake.

Had something actually happened to the airship? He scowled at the anxiety blooming abruptly in his stomach.

"Um. Shido…?" Yoshino said worriedly. Perhaps this look on his face made her uneasy.

"Ohhh… Sorry. Thanks," he said, and gave her phone back before turning toward the door. "I need your help. I don't know where we are. Can you lead me to a place I might recognize? Tohka and the others are in danger."

Yoshino and Natsumi looked stunned for a moment, but they quickly nodded their agreement with serious expressions on their faces.

"Ungh… Ngh…"

With a grimace, Tohka sat up. Apparently, she had passed out for a short while.

When she pressed a hand to her chest, she could feel the stickiness of matted blood. But this was no surprise. Whatever else, her Astral Dress, meant to be impenetrable armor, had been cruelly shredded by Origami's laser blade.

"I…," Tohka said, frowning.

"…Aah, Tohka… You're awaaaake?" came a weak voice in response. When she lifted her face, she caught sight of Miku in a tattered limited Astral Dress standing in front of Tohka as if to protect her, shoulders heaving. A number of cuts and blows marked her pale skin; she was truly battered and beaten. It was surprising she was still standing on her own two feet.

"Miku! A-are you okay?!"

"Yes… More or less. What about yo—?" Miku abruptly dropped to her knees and then slumped forward.

Tohka hurried over to support her. "Miku! Hang on!"

Miku smiled weakly, and her eyes slid shut. All the strength drained out of her body. She had fainted.

Tohka heard the sound of feet on rubble from up ahead. She turned her gaze in that direction to find the god of death standing there, clad in dull armor.

"Origami…Tobiichi!" She called the girl's name with hatred in her voice.

Origami turned cool eyes on her. Collapsed at her feet was Yuzuru, and a little farther away was Kaguya. They both appeared to still be conscious, but like Miku, they were grievously injured and so obviously in pain that Tohka unthinkingly wanted to avert her eyes.

All this indicated a fierce battle had taken place while Tohka was unconscious. Most likely to protect her defenseless self from Origami's hand.

Tohka gritted her teeth as she gently set Miku down before standing up with Sandalphon in her hands. "You… Why would you *do* this?!"

"I don't understand the question," Origami returned without so much as a flicker of emotion. "You are Spirits. World-killing catastrophes. The enemies of humanity. That alone is more than reason enough. Don't make me tell you again."

With the ultimate calm, Origami curled the fingers on her left hand upward, and the body of Yuzuru at her feet floated into the air, pulled by an invisible hand.

"An…guish. Master…Origami, why—?"

"…"

A faint crease sprang up on Origami's brow as she reached a hand out to Yuzuru's neck and interrupted her. She tightened her grip around Yuzuru's throat, and Yuzuru let out a pained cry.

Ignoring this, however, Origami held up the laser blade she gripped in her other hand, ready to plunge it into Yuzuru's stomach.

"You monster!" Tohka shouted, and raised Sandalphon before her.

But a heartbeat before she could swing her blade, a shadow came flying at Origami—Kaguya. After digging herself out from the rubble where she'd been facedown on the ground, Kaguya was bleeding copiously as she charged Origami with her enormous lance.

"What are you doing to Yuzuru, Origamiiiiiii?!" She charged with bloodshot eyes, looking like an actual demon.

Perhaps Origami was unable to fully respond to this abrupt attack; Kaguya's lance passed through her Territory and scratched part of the CR unit. But that was it.

"Ngh." Origami frowned slightly, and Kaguya's body fell to the earth as if pushed back by an invisible hand.

"Hngh!" Kaguya still didn't give up. She kept trying to hold her head high, but against the overwhelming power of the Territory, she was forced helplessly to the ground.

"Kaguya!"

The twins were in serious danger. That thought had barely finished crossing Tohka's mind when she launched herself toward Origami at top speed.

But long before she could reach the Wizard, Tohka stopped. More accurately, she *was* stopped, blocked by an invisible wall.

Origami had extended her Territory out to this range. With the freedom of movement ripped away from her, not only was Tohka unable to stop Origami, but she was also no longer even able to swing her sword.

"Hngh. Origami Tobiichi. You…!" she groaned, pained, but Origami appeared to pay this absolutely no mind as she readied her laser blade once more and turned her gaze on Yuzuru.

"It's been a long time. I finally have it. The power to defeat Spirits. The power to achieve my long-awaited goal," she said, as if reciting a monologue, and exhaled at length. It looked almost like she was breathing out the last uncertainty, expelling the final hesitation smoldering inside her.

"With this blow, I will get myself back. I will kill all the Spirits. So that there will never be another person like me born in this world," Origami said, as if to reassure herself, and her gaze grew sharper. She tightened her grip on the handle of her laser blade.

"Origami Tobiichi!" Tohka cried. But the Territory binding her didn't budge.

She couldn't give up, though. She was the only one there who could fight Origami now. The moment Tohka lowered her sword, Kaguya, Yuzuru, and Miku would be killed.

The way she was now, Origami could really do it. And Tohka had no doubt that once she murdered the Spirits, she would morph into a completely different being. Tohka didn't know why, but she absolutely could not allow that to happen.

"Ungh. Aaaaaaaaaaaaah!" she cried, and put everything she had into trying to break free of the Territory.

But it wasn't enough. This Territory, which boasted strength far beyond anything Origami had possessed before, did not so much as quiver.

She'd never break free like this. She couldn't save everyone in this state. She needed power. Much, much more power.

"…!"

The moment she realized this, she was overcome by an extreme chill.

She knew this sensation. This physical unease was incredibly similar to what she'd felt a few months earlier when Shido had been on the verge of being killed by Ellen at DEM's Japanese office.

A feeling of something other than herself had manifested inside her and taken her hand. Her own consciousness had grown weak, and in its place, an unfathomable blackness had filled her head, overwhelming her with a sense of terror.

Tohka gritted her teeth. She didn't know what that sensation was. But she instinctively guessed that she couldn't save everyone with that power.

She had to stay Tohka.

To save Kaguya.

To rescue Yuzuru.

To keep Miku alive.

And that girl.

In order to take the hand of the high-minded girl Tohka loathed, the girl who was arrogant, tyrannical, unsociable, foul-mouthed, whose thoughts Tohka never understood and who was always getting in Tohka's way.

Tohka had to swing her blade as Tohka.

"Shido! Give me strength!" She called Shido's name and tightened her hand around the hilt of her Angel, Sandalphon. "Aaaaaaaaa-aaaaaaaaaaaaaaaah!"

She had an image of something sparking inside her head and felt a warm sensation pouring into her body.

"...?!"

With her hand around the neck of Yuzuru Yamai, ready to run her sword through the Spirit's limp body, Origami frowned at the unexpected glow appearing ahead of her.

Tohka Yatogami's movement had been checked by Origami's Territory, but now she cried out, and her body began to shine with a dazzling light.

And the strangeness didn't stop there. Tohka had disappeared from the Territory holding her back.

No. That wasn't it. Origami was on guard now. It wasn't that Tohka had disappeared. The part of the Territory that had enveloped her had disappeared like a hole had been ripped through it.

"...!!"

In the next instant, Origami sensed an overpowering bloodlust and released Yuzuru's neck to leap backward.

A heartbeat later, a faintly glowing sword sliced through the spot where she had just been standing, leaving an afterimage of the path it traveled.

"Wha...?"

As Origami opened her eyes wide, baffled, a hand caught Yuzuru, who'd been about to drop to the ground now that she was free of Origami's Territory.

The light gradually subsided, and soon, Origami was able to see the owner of the hand.

The moment she caught sight of the girl who had appeared there, she gasped unconsciously.

Midnight hair tossed by the wind. Crystalline eyes staring quietly at her. Shining sword in one hand. Yes, this was Tohka Yatogami.

But the issue was what she was wearing.

Shoulders, chest, hips—bluish-purple armor covering every part of her body, with a faintly luminescent skirt. There was absolute majesty in her appearance, enough to overwhelm anyone who looked upon her. She was like an entirely different person from when she'd been trapped in Origami's Territory only moments ago.

Astral Dress. The absolute, most powerful armor and castle indicating that a Spirit was a Spirit.

This was not the limited version that Tohka had been wearing up to that point. Origami swallowed hard at this perfect and complete version of Tohka.

The last time she'd seen this had been more than six months ago. Before Tohka Yatogami had transferred to their school, she had nearly killed Origami on the plateau.

The sword Spirit, Princess, stood before her now.

"That dress...," Origami half murmured, the look on her face growing more severe.

Tohka set Yuzuru down next to Kaguya before lifting her face calmly. "Origami Tobiichi. I hate you. I did before, and I do now. But my hatred now is probably…a little different from the hatred before. So…"

She looked at Origami and pointed the tip of the Angel in her hand toward her.

"…I'm going to actually try to kill you. Don't die, Origami," Tohka said in a quiet but penetratingly icy tone.

"…!"

Just hearing these words, Origami felt a shot through the heart.

Overwhelming intimidation. An unrelenting pressure that almost pushed her to despair. A murderous rage assaulted her, and she knew that if she let her guard down for even the blink of an eye, her head would be taken from her shoulders and sent flying.

"…"

But Origami didn't pull back. In fact, this version of Tohka might have been exactly what she had been waiting for.

This was the most powerful Astral Dress, the very one that had knocked out the old Origami with a single blow. She felt like defeating Princess in her complete form would finally allow her to move forward.

"Haah!" With a fierce battle cry, Origami shrank her Territory to enclose only her body and her equipment and increased its strength. She wouldn't be able to bind Tohka's movements now by expanding its range anyway. In which case, it was more to her advantage to tighten her defense rather than pointlessly expend magic.

She swung her laser blade, and an arc of light swept toward Tohka.

The Spirit arched an eyebrow ever so slightly and stopped this with Sandalphon.

But that was exactly what Origami had been aiming for. She issued commands in her mind and split her laser blade.

Clarent, the main weapon of the DEM-made CR unit Mordred, could be changed into two different forms by varying the main body within a Territory: the magic gun Clarent Cannon and the laser blade Clarent Sword. But this change was merely to give the weapon a shape most suited to the different functions; it wasn't as though the weapon lost part of its power through transformation.

Although it required precision control of the Territory and vast magic generation, it was possible to fire the weapon as a gun while still maintaining the blade of the sword, depending on what you were trying to do. In other words, this was the way Origami was currently using it.

Magic streamed upward out of the gun barrel of the laser blade, which was locked in a struggle against Tohka's sword, before scattering into the sky and raining down on Tohka like a storm.

Of course, this blast came from Origami as she grappled with Tohka. It wasn't a particularly powerful shot, nothing more than pellets that could be easily knocked away with one swing from Sandalphon.

But Origami currently had Sandalphon pinned down. If Tohka tried to defend against the gun attack, she would instead taste the tip of Origami's blade. Either way, Tohka would not be able to escape injury.

Or she shouldn't have been about to anyway.

"Hah!"

But Tohka, still locked in a struggle with Origami, kicked at the ground and used overwhelming brute force to push Origami back and force an escape from the shower of bullets.

"Hngh!" Origami furrowed her brow and groaned. Tohka's Spirit power and incredible physical strength were indeed on a different level than they had been before. In terms of raw power, Origami didn't have a chance of winning.

She twisted her laser blade to deflect Tohka's sword before launching a series of attacks so blindingly fast that the eye couldn't keep up. Any one of these would have been enough to disintegrate a normal person. But Tohka's greatsword intercepted every last strike with impossible accuracy.

"Gaaah!" She thrust Sandalphon out, almost sliding the blade forward, at an opening in Origami's onslaught.

"Ngh…!"

But Origami saw this attack coming and stopped it.

Parry, slice, thrust, swing, stop, brandish.

The fighters each attacked relentlessly.

I can do this. Origami tightened her grip on Clarent.

In terms of actual ability, they were more or less evenly matched. Origami was no longer the girl who had been helplessly cut down by Tohka. With this new equipment, she could fight a full-blown Spirit.

Human intellect worked against world-killing catastrophes.

This was what Origami had wanted all these years, the hope she'd yearned for. She had not been wrong. Every bit of the training she'd undergone had not been in vain.

As long as she had the CR unit Mordred, Origami would be able to defeat Tohka Yatogami. And the Yamai sisters. And Miku Izayoi. And the Spirit who killed her parents five years ago.

Yes. The Spirit from five years ago. As a condition for joining DEM, Origami had obtained information on that Spirit from Ellen Mathers. Which was not to say that she now knew about the detailed appearance and abilities of this Spirit. As far as information went, she couldn't say it was worth too much.

But the DEM intel established that there had indeed been another Spirit besides Efreet / Kotori Itsuka there that day five years ago. For that alone, it had serious value.

Origami could do it as she was now. All she had to do was find that Spirit, and she could…

"Ah…?"

But then an intense pain stabbed into her head.

For a second, she wondered if she hadn't been able to completely defang Tohka's attack and she'd taken a blow to the head. But that wasn't it. This pain was clearly coming from *inside* her head.

Her consciousness began to flicker, and her field of vision was dyed red.

"Ah!"

"Haah!" Tohka did not let this chance slip away. She swung Sandalphon horizontally to slam the flat of the blade up against Origami's completely defenseless torso.

It was an absolutely tyrannical blow meant to purge anything and everything. Origami was helplessly knocked backward, like a leaf blown away by the wind.

She slammed into chunks of debris and rubble, went through the wall of a building, flying so far away from the battlefield now that she could no longer even see Tohka, and then bounced off the ground a few times before finally landing flat on her back.

"Hnnngh..."

She'd just barely managed to evade fatal injury because she'd tightened up her Territory, but the damage was serious. Contusions, lacerations. She was also bleeding profusely. If a passerby had seen her in this state, they would have immediately called an ambulance, whether she liked it or not.

But the serious injuries were not on the surface. Origami wiped her face with a hand and gritted her teeth at the reddish-black blood that came back stuck to it.

She was bleeding from her nose and her eyes. This wasn't the first time this had happened to her. This was the activation limit she'd seen when she'd pushed herself too far in her use of the destructive weapon White Licorice.

"Nnngh!"

To go up against Tohka after the Spirit had regained her complete powers, Origami had unknowingly overused her brain. She clenched her jaw, vexed, and punched the ground as she lay there on her back.

What was all that grand talk about being evenly matched? About being able to fight the Spirits?! In the end, Origami had done nothing more than barely keep up with Tohka all while shaving her own life away.

"I'm..."

She reached her trembling hand up toward the sky. Almost like a devout believer clinging to God.

Of course, she didn't believe in God. That day five years ago when

her parents had been killed before her very eyes, the word *God* had disappeared from her vocabulary.

But if…

…if God or the Devil had existed, Origami would no doubt have clung to that hand, no matter what she had to sacrifice. She'd have agreed to a contract that meant she would have to offer up her heart after achieving her objective.

She knew this thinking was not like her. Placing hope in something that didn't exist was the height of folly. The only one who could help you was you. If you had time to pray, you had time to train.

If you had time to wish, you had time to strategize. This was what had created the Wizard Origami Tobiichi.

Origami had nothing left now.

Training until she puked blood, studying instead of sleeping, cutting-edge equipment that forced her body to its limits, battle on the precipice of death. Origami had done everything she could possibly think of.

And the result of all that was this.

The power she'd given up everything to build was, in the end, not enough against a Spirit.

This harsh truth was the only thing waiting at the end of Origami's long fight.

"I am…"

A vision flitted through her head.

She exhaled weakly and let the hand held up to the heavens fall back lifelessly.

"Hey there. Don't you want to be stronger?"

Origami heard a voice in her ear that was neither man nor woman.

"Huh?" Her eyes grew wide at the sudden voice, and she pulled herself into a wobbling sitting position.

And saw *something* unfathomable standing there.

There was no other word to describe it. She could register that there was a presence before her, and yet she couldn't actually perceive it, almost like the resolution was poor. She even got the impression that its entire body was covered in static.

"You… What are you?" Without thinking, Origami used the word *what* rather than *who*.

Perhaps the something picked up on her confusion; she could hear a voice chuckling.

"It doesn't matter right now what I am. More important, what is your answer? Do you want power? Don't you want absolute power so you'll never lose to anyone again?"

"…!"

Origami gasped and furrowed her brow.

For a second, she wondered if the Realizer damage had knocked a screw loose in her head. This was clearly an unusual situation. Responding to a being like this was not the sane thing to do.

But her answer to the question was also blindingly obvious. Her consciousness fading, she opened her mouth.

"That's… Of course I do." She half spat the words. "I…want power. Whatever it takes. Whatever I have to sacrifice! I want the absolute power I need to achieve my heart's desire! Enough power so that no one can touch me… I want *all* the power!"

"You do?" the something said briefly in response.

It was strange. Even though she couldn't see its face, Origami felt like the something grinned for an instant.

"In that case, I'll give it to you. All the power you want," it said, and held an object out to her.

The object appeared to be glowing white. For a moment, she was lost in that mesmerizing shine. "This…"

"If you want power, hold out your hand."

"…"

Even as she frowned dubiously, Origami slowly did as she was told and touched the gem.

"Wha…?!"

The gem flashed dazzlingly bright, floated up into the air, and was absorbed into her chest.

"What…is…?" she muttered, stunned, as she looked down at herself, but the gem was no longer there. "What was—?" She started to ask, lifting her face, but then stopped. The something, which had been before her only half a second ago, had vanished without a trace.

"…"

So had she just hallucinated everything because of how badly she'd been hit? Origami assumed that must be the case and put a hand to her forehead.

But then…

"Uh…?"

…her heart pounded loudly, and she furrowed her brow. It felt like she had an entirely new heart in her body, pumping blood hotter than what had been originally flowing through her veins. She fell to her knees at the completely abnormal and unprecedented sensation.

"Ah. Aaah. Aaaaaaaaaaaaaaaaaaaaaaaaaaaaaaaaaaaaaaaaaaaaaaaaah! Ah! Ah!"

As her consciousness faded, Origami felt like she was being reborn as something else.

"…! What's is it?!" AST Captain Ryouko Kusakabe cried out when an alarm abruptly sounded at the SDF Tengu Garrison.

Normally, the AST were training at this time of day, but Ryouko was in the control room due to certain circumstances.

The technician tapped at her console and then let out a squeak. "I-it's…an incredible Spirit signal!"

"A Spirit signal… Is this DEM again?!" Ryouko scowled.

They had measured several Spirit signals very recently, in fact.

Berserk, Diva…and Princess.

The signal from Princess, in particular, had suddenly increased after the initial measurement, indicating the same level of power as when they'd fought her previously.

The reason that Ryouko and the rest of the Spirit-hunting AST were just sitting around while so many Spirits appeared in the city was exceedingly simple—DEM Industries. The company put serious pressure on the Ministry of Defense to keep the AST from interfering when they were carrying out special operations.

Thus, Ryouko and her team could only glare at the radar in the control room, all the while knowing that Spirits were manifesting in Tengu.

Eyes glued to the digits on the screen, the technician swallowed hard, looking scared. "N-no…! This isn't one of the ones mentioned in the DEM briefing!"

"What did you say?!" Ryouko cried as she set her hands on the technician's shoulders and peered at the screen.

Indeed, she did see there a Spirit signal different from the ones of the Spirits they'd witnessed so far. And the numbers were far too powerful, on par with Princess at full strength.

"You're telling me that a *different* Spirit showed up during the operation? And given that there's no spacequake, it's a quiet manifestation?!"

Ryouko's face grew stern. To say that this was a situation that required emergency action was an understatement. If this Spirit began to fight with Princess, she couldn't begin to estimate how much damage there would be.

"Captain!"

The door to the control room flew open, and two small girls came inside. AST member Mikie Okamine and mechanic Mildred F. Fujimura. Mikie was already wearing her wiring suit.

"All AST personnel are ready to go!" she said.

"CR units are in top shape, too," the mechanic continued. "Full performance whenever you need it."

"Mikie… Milly…," Ryouko said their names with a sigh.

There was no way they could have responded this quickly to a Spirit signal that had only just been detected. Most likely, they'd been preparing to mobilize for a while now. Because they felt the same way she did.

When Origami was disciplined, Mikie had been so upset that she'd announced that she was going to quit the AST, too. And now here she was, magnificently fulfilling her duty. She was pushing herself so that she could hold her head high when Origami came back one day. Ryouko's expression softened at this growth in her subordinate.

"Captain!" the technician called out. "Message from headquarters!"

"Huh! Good timing." Ryouko assumed it was probably a mobilization order, and she pulled the emergency device out of her pocket.

However.

"Er. It says for the AST…to continue on standby."

Ryouko, Mikie, and Milly opened their eyes wide in surprise.

"Wh-what are they thinking?" Ryouko demanded. "A Spirit has manifested in the city!"

"I—I know, but…" The technician looked troubled. And well, yes, of course she was. She was only relaying the order from on high.

"Argh!" Ryouko clenched her jaw, frustrated, and slammed a fist into the wall. "What is the point of the AST if we're not mobilized in an emergency like this? Are those idiots at headquarters this scared of DEM?!"

Origami's face flitted through her mind. She may have had a lot of issues as a team member, but the one thing she would never do was go against her own principles. If she had been at the scene, she would have certainly ignored the standby order and mobilized without hesitating.

But if Ryouko did that here, her superiors would no doubt gleefully replace her as captain. Most likely with an easier-to-control Wizard backed by DEM. She had to avoid that at all cost.

"C-Captain…" Mikie had a worried look on her face.

After agonizing for a few seconds, Ryouko spat, "All hands, continue to standby!"

"Kaguya! Yuzuru! Are you okay?!"

Tohka raced over to the Yamai sisters on the ground after sending Origami flying with a single blow from Sandalphon.

She could have followed up her attack on Origami, but she didn't. Her aim had never been to kill the other girl. Her top priority now was to make sure that Kaguya and the others were okay.

Kaguya pulled herself up, and Yuzuru waved a limp hand. Their wounds were anything but shallow, though at the very least, they were still conscious. Tohka let out a sigh of relief.

"Tohka... That dress," Kaguya murmured, pushing back the pain, as she turned her gaze on Tohka, staring with fascination at her outfit.

Tohka raised a curious eyebrow at first, but she soon realized why Kaguya was staring. Manifested on Tohka's body at that moment was a complete Astral Dress.

"Mm," she said. "I felt like I just *had* to rescue you, and the power came back to me."

Kaguya looked over her Astral Dress one more time before pursing her lips and thrusting them forward. "Dang, that's so cool. How did you yank out that much power at the last minute like a superhero? The retainer is more remarkable than the master. You gotta tell me how to do that later."

"Mm. Sure," Tohka assented automatically, but she couldn't really explain how she did it. She herself didn't understand how her Spirit power, which was supposed to be locked away in Shido, had suddenly returned to her.

"*Cough! Cough!*" Yuzuru sat up a moment later and coughed painfully a few times. "Question... Tohka, where's Master Origami...?"

Tohka nodded firmly. "I hit her as hard as I could with the flat of my blade. She probably won't be able to fight for a while, but she won't die. Pretty sure she's got that teriyaki thing around her body, so."

She thrust the tip of Sandalphon into the ground, and Kaguya and Yuzuru cocked their heads to the sides, mirror opposites.

"Teriyaki?"

"Correction. Do you mean Territory?" Yuzuru said. And now that she mentioned it, Tohka felt like that *was* maybe the name of it.

"Right. That terry-toe-ree thing."

"" ...?""

She thought she'd gotten it right this time for sure, but for some reason, the Yamai sisters still seemed confused.

But she didn't have time to get into that now. Tohka looked away from the Yamai sisters to check behind them.

Miku was lying there on the smashed-up road.

"Miku!" she called, but got no response. It seemed that Miku still hadn't regained consciousness. Tohka ran over to her, knelt down, and peered at her face.

But in contrast to her expectations, what she found there was a remarkably relaxed expression. Miku's breathing was slow and even, and from time to time, she even muttered to herself in her sleep. Tohka let out a sigh of relief.

"Keh-keh! Upon her awakening, you would do best to express your gratitude, Tohka. That one put her body on the line to guard you as you lay unconscious."

"Assent. She was magnificent. Although, her legs were trembling from start to finish."

Kaguya and Yuzuru followed Tohka to Miku's side, holding each other up.

"Mm. Right. Thanks, Miku," Tohka said.

"Ah yes. Thus, it is best to awaken her quickly."

"Mm? How do I do that?" Tohka asked.

"Keh-keh! The truth here is well-known. The awakening of a sleeping princess requires a passionate kiss."

"A-a kiss?!"

"Affirmation. She is correct. Now, go ahead and give it everything you have. Kiss. Kiss."

"M-mm..." If that was the only way, then Tohka really had no choice, did she? She swallowed hard.

"Halt! I said nothing!"

"Conformity. Neither did Yuzuru."

"Wh-what?!"

The twins cried out, and Tohka furrowed her brow. Now that they mentioned it, she did feel like the voices she'd just heard were a *little* different from those of the twins. In which case...

She dropped her eyes to find Miku grinning, her eyes open just a crack.

"Ah! Miku!" she cried as she thrust out an accusatory finger. "You were awake?!"

"Pffft! Ha-ha-ha! Aaah, you caught meeee?" Miku burst out laughing like she could no longer hold it in. It seems that she had actually been awake. "And boo to you, Kaguya, Yuzuru! Why'd you have to say anything? Another second or two and I could have had my fiiill of Tohka's pretty lips!"

"How brazenly you speak such shameful things! The crime of impersonating our voice is a grave one, Miku! Know that your sin will not be atoned for even should you fall into the pits of hell!"

"Outrage. That is arrrgh."

Kaguya and Yuzuru complained loudly with stern looks on their faces.

Miku yanked herself into a sitting position and touched their feet showily.

"I'm sorry. I didn't mean iiit. Please forgive me. I'll make it up to you with my boooody," she said as she licked her lips.

All color drained from the faces of the Yamai sisters, and they stepped back, as if fleeing Miku.

"Aaah, why are you running awaaaay? Please wait!"

"S-silence! Do not approach, deviant!"

"Escape. No cooties."

Miku chased after them, and the twins staggered back to try and evade her. It was an impossibly peaceful scene, as if the lethal battle they'd just been a part of was all a bad dream.

Tohka relaxed when she saw the three girls so full of life, and then she clapped her hands as if announcing their stumbling game of tag was over.

"At any rate, you're all badly injured," Tohka said. "You have to be treated on *Fraxinus*. Can someone call Kotori?"

The girls finally stopped their little game and turned their eyes on Tohka.

"Keh-keh! Shall we, then? Well, such wounds are a mere trifle to one such as I, but there is the question of the others."

"Mischief. Pew-pew."

"Eeeaaaugh?!"

Yuzuru poked the cut on Kaguya's stomach, and Kaguya shrieked, tears springing up in her eyes. The pain was indeed real.

"Wh-what are you doing?!" she yelled.

"Sneer. I'm not doing anything. (Snark.)"

"Ooh! I want to do that, toooo! Pew-pew!"

"Hey! Quit it! Come on already!"

The three started to squabble once again, and Tohka sighed.

"Anyway, please just do it. You all go on ahead to *Fraxinus*."

"Go on ahead?" Miku arched a curious eyebrow. "What are youuu going to do, Tohka?"

"Mm," she said. "I'm going to go get Origami Tobiichi and bring her in. She probably can't move without some help. And she still hasn't told me what's going on."

The Spirits sighed before nodding in agreement.

"Hmm. If you say it will be so, Tohka, then we shall trust in you. Naturally, whatever her reasons, we shall indeed make her pay properly the price of this transgression."

"Assent. The punishment is tickle hell. We will break Master Origami's iron mask."

"Oh! For this payment, would a private roooom be okay? There are all kinds of things I'd like to do," Miku said, eyes shining.

Sweat beaded on Kaguya's and Yuzuru's foreheads.

After confirming that they agreed, Tohka turned her gaze in the direction she had sent Origami flying. She'd been pretty angry, so she might have used too much force. She couldn't even see her from here...

"Mm?" Tohka's eyebrows jumped up.

Directly ahead, she saw something that looked like a human silhouette against the gray clouds that blanketed the sky.

"Is something wrong, Tohka?" Kaguya asked.

"Oh..." Tohka was pressed for a response and narrowed her eyes. For a second, she thought she'd been seeing things, but no.

A beam of light cut through the gloomy sky, a girl hanging in the center of it.

The first thing Tohka noticed was the outfit, of course.

The dress clung to the girl's body, with a large, wide skirt like a flower in full bloom. A ring floated in a perfect circle around her head, a veil of light stretching down from it. Everything was so white, it could wake the dead.

It was almost like Shinto bridalwear that only the purest of maidens could wear. Or like an angel descending from the heavens.

"...! That's—" Tohka wasn't gasping because she was dazzled by these elements. As the white silhouette slowly approached, she was finally able to get a good look at the girl's face.

The face of Origami Tobiichi.

"Origami...?"

"Confirmation. So that's who it looks like to you, too, Kaguya?"

"Riiight. Hmm? But that look..."

Kaguya, Yuzuru, and Miku had also noticed this girl. They spoke one after the other, brows furrowed.

But their conversation ended very quickly.

Because as Origami turned toward them with languid eyes, they were overcome with a powerful chill, countless needles stabbing into their bodies.

"...!"

Kaguya, Yuzuru, and Miku opened their eyes wide in surprise and stood rooted to the spot, stunned. Tohka gritted her teeth and stepped in front of the three Spirits, brandishing Sandalphon, as if to put a barrier between them and Origami.

"T-Tohka!" Kaguya said.

"Run," she replied without taking her eyes off Origami for even a split second. Sweat dripped down her forehead, crossed her cheeks, and dripped from her chin. "I can't fight *and* protect you."

Kaguya and the other girls did not object. No one exclaimed that they would stay and fight. They had likely realized that they would be of no help whatsoever, given that none of them had full access to their Spirit power. Not only would they be helpless, but they were also very likely to become liabilities.

That was simply how dangerous this overwhelming power was. They had no need to cross swords with her, no need to speak to her; they understood instinctively. *This* was something they could not stand against.

"Apologies, Tohka!"

"Prayer. I wish you success in battle."

"Oh! Hey, you two— Gaaah!"

Kaguya and Yuzuru each grabbed one of Miku's arms, wrapped the wind around them, and escaped into the sky at terrific speed.

"…"

Origami showed no interest in them. She simply stared at Tohka as she glided slowly through the air toward her. And then looking down on the Spirit, she parted her lips.

"Tohka…Yatogami. I will. Defeat you."

"Origami. You!" Tohka cried, her gaze sharp on the girl in the sky.

Origami leisurely raised a hand to the heavens. And then she shouted the name of an Angel she could not have known.

"Metatron."

Several beams of light shot down from the dark evening sky and wrapped around her. These beams gradually took on physical form as long, thin, mechanical feathers.

Origami clenched the hand she had brandished above her head, and the feathers came together to overlap in a circle. Like a crown being set upon her head.

"Ngh…" Tohka grimaced.

An Astral Dress…and an Angel. There was no mistaking it now.

"Origami…," she called, face still turned upward. "Why are you a Spirit now?!"

She didn't know what had happened while she'd been helping

Kaguya, Yuzuru, and Miku. But one thing was certain—Origami had become a Spirit.

"Spi...rit...," Origami murmured, as if repeating Tohka, and listlessly looked down at her hand, at her body. "So...I really am. But...it doesn't matter."

Her eyes flew open, and she turned a gaze like a sword on Tohka.

"I wield this power to defeat the Spirits. I became a Spirit to kill the Spirits. I will subjugate all Spirits. And I will also disappear when I am the last Spirit remaining."

She threw her arms out, and the tips of the crown on her head extended to form a circle like the sun.

"Metatron. Shemesh," she announced quietly.

Instantly, the circular Angel began to spin around her head, scattering particles of light in all directions.

"Ngh!" Tohka threw out a hand to raise a defensive wall with her Spirit power. A heartbeat later, the overwhelming shower of light from Origami's Angel poured down around her.

It was terribly beautiful, terribly violent rain. Countless droplets of Spirit energy, each and every one containing incomprehensible power, showered the earth and crushed everything beneath them.

The asphalt road. The abandoned cars. The neat rows of houses. The impartial Angel did not distinguish among them. The familiar residential neighborhood crumbled helplessly in the face of this power, like a paper model in the rain.

"Hngh!" Tohka's wall of Spirit power withstood the attack somehow, but she wouldn't get anywhere standing behind it. She tightened her grip on Sandalphon and stepped forward, knowing full well she would suffer countless blows as she did.

"Aaaaaaaaah!" She swung Sandalphon with a fierce cry, and the slicing attack shot out, tracing the length of her blade.

"...!"

Origami twitched an eyebrow, and she held a hand out downward. The light-emitting ring split and reformed as a shield in front of her to repel Tohka's attack.

Then for an instant, the particles of light broke apart. Not letting this opportunity pass her by, Tohka kicked off the ground and leaped straight up into the air, slipping past the Angel to close in on Origami.

"Hyaaaaaah!" She couldn't hold back here. She gripped Sandalphon with both hands and swung it at Origami with everything she had.

However, she felt no impact.

The moment Sandalphon touched her Astral Dress, Origami became light and vanished, only to reappear a few meters behind where she had been.

"Wha…?!"

"…!"

Tohka wasn't the only one whose eyes flew open in surprise. Origami was supposedly the one who had evaded the attack, but her face was also twisted up in what looked like shock. It seemed that she hadn't expected this sequence of events, either.

She stared at her own hands and half spat the word, "Monster." Frowning, she clenched one of those hands into a fist and then thrust it up into the air. "Mal'akh!"

Metatron converged on her back to create what looked like wings. Origami moved the Angel in a flapping motion and broke away to her rear.

At the same time, beams of light shot out from the tips of the Metatron wings and closed in on Tohka.

"What…?!" Tohka cried out, and swung Sandalphon. It was too late to put up a defensive wall, and she instinctively guessed that her wall wouldn't be able to completely defend against this attack anyway.

She knocked away the approaching beams of light with her Angel. But there were too many. The beams she missed stabbed into her shoulder and leg.

"Hnnngh!"

What intense pain. She didn't have to look to know that her Astral Dress had been shot through.

But Origami didn't let up. She brought the hand in the air down, and the wings on her back scattered in all directions.

"Kadour!" she shouted, and the pieces of Metatron spun around in the sky on their own independent trajectories, shooting light from all directions.

Imprisonment in a cage of light particles. And this was a violent jail, cutting through flesh and bone if touched.

"Ngh!" Tohka swung her sword to knock away the successive blows.

But it was impossible to deal with the whole barrage. Her back, her hip, her hand. The light, with lethal intentionality, struck and pierced her armor.

"Hnnngh, ungh. Ah!"

The fight was too one-sided; she was the only one being tortured. With a grimace of anguish, she glared at Origami and launched herself into the air.

To block this charge, Metatron threw even fiercer attacks at her, but she completely ignored them. A direct hit to her stomach and her leg didn't stop Tohka and she furiously charged, never taking her eyes off Origami.

"Aaaaaaaaaaaaaaaaah!" she cried, and swung Sandalphon at the other girl. "Kah!"

There was again no impact communicated from her sword to her hands. Her blade was on the verge of slicing through Origami when the new Spirit disappeared in a flash of light to evade it. A heartbeat later, her body recomposed itself in a spot a little ways off, just like the last time.

But Tohka had factored that into her calculations. She dropped Sandalphon, and with the momentum of her charge, she twisted in the air.

"Yaaaaaah!!"

With her bare hands and all the strength in her body, she punched at Origami's head where it had rematerialized.

"Ngh. Hah…?!" Origami groaned and screwed her face up. A white something—maybe a tooth—flew out of her mouth.

A straight right with all the might of the fully powered Spirit Tohka behind it. If Origami hadn't turned into a Spirit, then instead of knocking her head right off, this blow probably would've smashed it to smithereens.

Perhaps she was unable to repeatedly transform into light. Or maybe she couldn't adequately respond to an attack she couldn't see coming. Tohka didn't know exactly the whys of it, but at any rate, she had succeeded in landing a blow. She clenched her fist tightly and sniffed triumphantly.

But any further follow-up attacks were out of the question. Even as Origami shook her head hazily, she was turning Metatron back into wings and retreating at top speed.

"Tch!" Tohka dropped back down to the ground and held her right hand out to her side. A few seconds later, Sandalphon fell from the sky and settled neatly into it.

"…"

She looked up at Origami, who was wiping blood away from her mouth.

Tohka had done a decent bit of damage, but her own injuries were clearly worse. If the fight kept going like this, Tohka would be at a disadvantage. She had no moves left.

In which case, there was only one thing for her to do.

"Sandalphon!" She called the name of her Angel and slammed a heel into the ground.

The name wasn't only for the sword she held in her hand.

The ground swelled up, and an enormous throne rose up, far taller than Tohka herself.

"Halvanhelev!" she shouted.

Her Angel Sandalphon's true form, the name of the most powerful sword.

Cracks raced across the throne, and the majestic seat broke apart into pieces. Those fragments wrapped around the sword Tohka held to form a new blade.

Origami would be able to dodge a single blow with her curious light-transformation ability. And she wasn't so stupid as to be caught by the same trick twice.

Kotori or Reine probably would have come up with a better strategy. No doubt they would have analyzed Origami's abilities and taken the most efficient approach to the fight.

But Tohka couldn't do that. All she knew was the feedback she felt with her sword and her fist. The only thing she could come up with was an extremely ungainly plan based on that—the ultimate attack to massacre Origami in the place she fled to as particles of light.

"Ngh..."

Perhaps Origami had sensed this new resolve in Tohka. She returned Metatron from its wing state to the original, then tuned its tips in Tohka's direction.

Tohka could more or less guess what this meant. An Angel with the power to rip through an Astral Dress with a single shot. This would be the ultimate blow, bundling all those light beams.

"Origami!" Tohka lifted her voice to the sky. "I'll ask you just one more time! Can we really not see eye to eye here?!"

"...! Don't be ridiculous," Origami responded, her face twisting up grimly. For some reason, to Tohka, she looked exactly like a small child about to start crying. "My intention hasn't changed. My mission hasn't changed. I reject all Spirits!"

Tohka took a deep breath. "Yeah? I guess we're doing this, then."

She slowly raised Halvanhelev. The blade was shrouded in inky-black light.

"I'm going to seriously rake you over the coals. Here I come, you sulky brat!"

"Keep dreamiiiiiing!" Origami yelled, and raised both hands in front of her. A pure-white light began to coalesce in the center of Metatron.

"Sandalphon. Halvanhelev!"

"Metatron. Artelif!"

Their shouts came at the same time.

Shining light in the heavens.

Dark glow of the earth.

Ready to launch from above and below, these attacks contained the full force of each of their Spirit power.

But at that moment.

"Stoppppppppppp!"

A desperate scream reached their ears.

"Wha…?!"

"…!"

Tohka and Origami gasped in surprise at the same time and turned to look in the direction of the voice.

It was a far cry from a sane move to avert their eyes in the middle of a battle, not to mention one in which their opponent had more than enough power to kill them. But this voice alone was one that neither Tohka nor Origami could ignore. Because…

"Shido!"

"Shido?!"

Both girls' eyes flew open in surprise.

The supposedly missing Shido Itsuka himself had arrived.

"What the…? How did this even happen?!" he shouted, scowling. "Tohka! Origami!"

"Shido, what are you…?" Origami muttered, stunned, as she averted her face. Almost as if she didn't want him to see her like this.

"Ngh…"

She switched Metatron from a crown to wings and shot off into the distant sky.

"Origami! Origamiiiiiiiiiiiii!"

Leaving only Shido's cry behind.

Chapter 4
Deadly Truth

A few minutes after flying away from the demolished residential area, Origami finally slackened her pace when she reached a patch of high ground with not a soul in sight.

"..."

She glanced back, but it seemed that no one had come after her. Silently, she flicked a hand upward and disassembled the Angel Metatron, affixed to her in the shape of wings, before dropping down to the ground.

Her brow furrowing slightly, she watched as Metatron split into its individual components, the ties binding it undone; the Angel dissolved into particles of light and melted into the air.

It was a curious sensation. Origami had intuitively mastered the unusual object, a thing she hadn't even known existed an hour ago, with the same ease as a weapon she'd been using for years.

It disturbed her. After the gem from the static something was absorbed into her body, she'd instinctively known how to operate the Angel. And that wasn't all. When she'd wanted to evade Tohka's attack before, she felt her own body instantly turn to light. She had transformed into something that could no longer be called human.

"What is this power?" she murmured, words likely not to be heard by anyone else, and dropped her gaze to the snowy-white garment wrapped around her.

The absolute armor of a Spirit.

Yes. What Origami was wearing was, without a doubt, an Astral Dress.

"I'm...a Spirit...," she muttered, and clenched her jaw to hold back the feeling of nausea that welled up in her from the depths of her stomach.

An extreme sense of loathing washed over her at the fact that she had become the thing she most hated, despised, detested.

This was also the reason why she'd fled the battleground even when her decisive fight against Tohka Yatogami was finally at hand. The instant Shido had appeared there, the hatred toward herself that had been numbed by the battle reared its ugly head.

Shido was the one person of all people she didn't want seeing her in this form. That was the final indulgence left to her after she'd pursued power at whatever the cost—her little selfish desire.

But there was something much more important for her to be worried about at the moment. It went without saying that this was the staticky something that had turned Origami into a Spirit.

"It can't be..."

Turning a human being into a Spirit. As unbelievable as this ability was, Origami had actually heard of it before.

Shido had told her about a mysterious presence, a strange something that had changed the once-human Kotori Itsuka into a Spirit. The other Spirit who had been there in the burning city on that day five years ago.

This static-like being had that exact ability.

"Was that...Phantom...?"

Phantom, the code name for the unidentified Spirit in Shido's tale.

She had no proof that what she saw today was the same Phantom that had appeared before Shido and Kotori five years earlier. To start with, humanity simply had too little information on the Spirits. They didn't even know if there was only one such Spirit with the power to turn humans into Spirits.

But if this static-something was the same Spirit that had materialized five years earlier in the Nanko neighborhood of Tengu, then…

"It…killed my mom and dad…?"

This meant that this unknown something was the reason her parents were dead.

She couldn't interrogate the something because they had already disappeared by the time this possibility had dawned on her. What she needed to do now was hunt them down somehow and investigate their objectives and true identity. And where they had been on that day five years earlier.

"Ungh…!"

Once her thoughts reached that point, Origami was overcome with nausea a second time and grimaced.

It wasn't only the fact that she had become a Spirit. The fact that she had been turned into one by the being that might be responsible for her parents' deaths became an odious sludge that cloaked her heart.

She somehow managed to resist the desire to drop to her knees and forced herself to look ahead.

She didn't know why the something had given her Spirit power. Or what their aim was. Or why they'd chosen Origami. Maybe they just went around making more Spirits on a whim.

She was certain of one thing alone, however.

She was a Spirit now. And she had the power to defeat Spirits.

The standard AST equipment. The destructive weapon White Licorice. The specialized CR unit Mordred. All these different devices had never been able to bring her to the heights she sought, and now here she was at last.

Absolute power was finally in her grasp. It was more than enough power to go toe to toe with the Spirit Princess, aka Tohka Yatogami, even after Tohka had regained her full abilities.

Origami had obtained the power she had yearned for so desperately and endlessly, albeit in the absolute worst possible form.

"The way I am now…"

Could defeat the Spirits.

And not just Phantom. Tohka Yatogami. Yoshino. Kotori Itsuka. Kaguya Yamai. Yuzuru Yamai. Miku Izayoi. Natsumi. And above all else, even Kurumi Tokisaki.

"… Ah." Her eyes flew open.

A thought flashed through her mind. A possibility. Nothing more than her own selfish pipe dream. She had no proof she could make it happen. In fact, the chances of success were extremely low.

But it meshed so perfectly. The Spirit power she had gained was the final piece of the puzzle that could complete the picture of this potentiality.

"If… If something like this is possible…" She got goose bumps all over. It was different from the hatred she'd felt before. This was a sensation resembling excitement, the feeling of a person long suffering, wandering lost in a deep, dark cave, and then finding a single beam of light pushing through a crack in the rock.

"…"

Origami swallowed hard and took a step forward.

She had to look for a certain person.

"A-are you okay, Tohka?" Shido asked.

"Mm. It's nothing serious." Tohka nodded firmly, covered in cold compresses and bandages. But perhaps that movement pulled at the cuts on her stomach; she furrowed her brow and groaned. "Unnngh… Mm."

"Hey, come on," he scolded her. "I told you not to push it. You gotta rest a while."

"Mm. I will." She obediently lay back on the bed.

They were in the nurse's office on the first floor of Raizen High School. They were initially going to head to Shido's house or to the apartment building where the Spirits lived, but that area had been ripped apart by the battle between Tohka and Origami, so they'd had no other choice but to come here.

Lying on the beds around the room were Tohka, and also Kaguya, Yuzuru, and Miku, who had joined up with them after Origami left. They had also fought Origami alongside Tohka early on.

The worst of the bleeding had been staunched using Natsumi's abilities, but for the actual healing itself, they could only rely on their own physical strength. Like Tohka, the other three fighters had bandages all over, so they looked like mummies, turning the nurse's room into a king's tomb sealed from ancient times.

The only equipment in the room were bandages, disinfectants, and compresses. With no nurse and no health teacher, the only first-aiders were Shido, Yoshino, and Natsumi. But beggars couldn't be choosers.

After Origami left, they'd tried to get in touch with *Fraxinus* to have them treat Tohka, who was badly injured but they still hadn't managed to get through to them on the phone.

"Um. Are they okay?" Yoshino asked, a worried look on her face, as she gently wiped Kaguya's dirt-covered face with a damp cloth.

"Whoa, you really got your butt handed to you!" her puppet followed up.

Kaguya grimaced in pain, but she quickly recovered her cool, the expression on her face trying to communicate that this was nothing, really nothing at all. Although, the faintest of tears did spring up in the corners of her eyes.

"Exhalation. Kaguya is playing tough," Yuzuru said from one side.

"Sh-shut up! It doesn't hurt at all!" Kaguya responded almost automatically. But it apparently really did hurt. She screwed up her face and lay back against the bed once more.

"Ha-ha!" Shido smiled slightly. If she still had the energy to be this stubborn, then she was probably going to be okay.

Meanwhile, Natsumi, after having half forced out her Spirit power to staunch everyone's wounds, was holding her knees to her chest and muttering in a corner. Somehow, he felt like the lighting was a bit darker in just that part of the room. She'd probably had to conjure up some serious mental trauma in order to treat everyone.

"Ow ow ow," Miku muttered to herself as she sat up on the bed against the wall.

"What's wrong, Miku? You shouldn't push yourself." Shido started toward her, and Miku held out the palm of her hand as if to stop him.

"I'm aaaall right. And while I still have some Spirit power left, there's a job I really haaave to do."

"A job?" Shido raised an eyebrow.

Miku nodded firmly as she snapped a hand out and clapped her fingers against her thumb, like she was playing a castanet.

"Gabriel. Requiem."

A number of silver pipes manifested around her. They were part of her Angel, Gabriel.

Everyone opened their eyes wide in shock, while Miku grinned and bowed neatly.

"Ladies and, um, gentleman. Welcome to this special one-night-only performance. Miku Izayoi on stage!" she said, took a deep breath, and made her beautiful voice fill the air. As if in resonance with that, Gabriel moved, and the sound grew even louder.

"Mm. What's this?"

"Oh-ho…"

"Admiration. The pain is less now."

With wide eyes, Tohka and the Yamai sisters looked down at themselves.

"Ha-ha-ha!" Miku smiled. "It's a song with a painkiller effect. It can't actually heal you, though. At best, it will make you rest a little easier."

"No, this is great, thanks. I feel a lot better." Tohka sighed and relaxed.

Shido also let out a relieved sigh.

But they definitely couldn't be optimistic about the situation they found themselves in. Not with *Fraxinus* incommunicado and DEM maneuvering behind the scenes.

"Hey, tell me something. What on earth happened with her, with Origami?" Shido asked Tohka, the Yamai sisters, and Miku, somehow managing to keep his voice from trembling with tension.

When he ran onto the battlefield, Tohka was using the massive

Halvanhelev not against a Wizard in a DEM CR unit, but against a Spirit dressed in a snowy-white Astral Dress and brandishing an Angel.

Seeing Tohka wielding power that was supposedly locked away had for sure been a surprise. But seeing the other girl so unexpectedly in the air there had pushed the confusion in his head to its maximum.

Origami had originally been a human being. In other words, that day and in the middle of fighting Tohka, she had become a Spirit. That was the only possible explanation.

It was a preposterous, unbelievable story. But Shido couldn't laugh it off. Whatever else, he had seen the Spirit-ified Origami with his own eyes.

Actually, to be more precise, that wasn't the only reason he believed this unbelievable story.

He knew of a Spirit that turned humans into Spirits.

Phantom.

The being that had appeared before Shido and Kotori five years earlier and transformed Kotori into the Spirit Efreet. The being that, for whatever reason, had hidden their own memories from them. And the being that may very well have killed Origami's parents.

If his guess was correct, Origami had encountered this Phantom and been turned into a Spirit herself.

In which case, Tohka and the others who'd been fighting Origami might have seen Phantom, too. Swallowing hard, he looked at the faces of each of those four Spirits in turn.

However.

"Aah, I don't know what happened. I knocked her flying, and then when she came back, she was already like that," Tohka said, a troubled look on her face. Kaguya and Yuzuru nodded along, similar expressions on their own faces.

"Hmph, it was indeed a thunderbolt. Keh! That ostentatious entrance! Is there not something I might reference there...? No, but white does not particularly complement me..."

"Assent. It was incredibly intimidating. If Tohka hadn't used her full Spirit power, we might have all been done for."

But while the other Spirits knew nothing, Miku was tapping a finger to her chin, like she had thought of something.

"Hmm. I didn't seeeee her, but...what if Origami also met God?"

That reminded him. Like Kotori, Miku had also been turned from a human being into a Spirit by a Spirit that was likely Phantom. It was actually only natural that she might land on this reason being the cause of Origami's abrupt transformation.

"Maybe," Shido replied in a quiet voice, and silently set his mind to work.

He didn't know what had happened to Origami. But it was an unmistakable fact that she had become one of the Spirits she hated so vehemently.

He remembered the look on Origami's face when she saw Shido and flew off in the sky. The face of the girl who loathed the Spirits.

What kinds of emotions were swirling around in her heart as she carried this impossible paradox in herself? At the very least, there was no doubting that she was wracked with such anguish that Shido couldn't even begin to imagine it. This upset his own heart almost more than he could bear.

"So what's Origami going to do now, then?" he said, almost to himself, and Tohka raised her voice, like she had just remembered something.

"Now that I'm thinking about it, she said that she'd use the power of Spirits to kill Spirits. And then in the end...she'd even kill herself, too."

"...!"

A shiver ran up Shido's spine.

If he was honest, this was within the realm of his expectations. As a possible worst case.

"Origami..." He had to get some clue to her whereabouts sooner rather than later. Impatience made his heart pound faster.

But not only was he in no position to go after her at that moment, the reality of the situation was also that he didn't even have any way of finding out where she was. *Fraxinus* might have been able to search for Origami with autonomous cameras and various sensors, but given that he couldn't get in touch with the airship, he had no way of confirming that.

"Ngh!" He gritted his teeth in frustration. The fact that he wasn't able to contact *Fraxinus* meant that he was simply stuck here like this.

The whole thing made him aware all over again of how much he normally relied on Kotori and Reine. Still, he couldn't exactly sit there and do nothing. He exhaled slowly and took stock of what needed to be done.

"At any rate, we have to get you all fixed up first and foremost. The alarm'll probably be turned off soon, so when it is, we'll head to the hospital. All we can do here is give you some first aid, so you need an actual doctor to have a look at you."

He needed to deal with Origami, too, but this took priority. But then he realized something else on his list.

"Oh...," he said quietly, turning his eyes toward Tohka.

Now that he was thinking about it, when he'd raced over to the scene of the battle, Tohka had fully manifested her Astral Dress. Which meant that unlike with the other three Spirits in their limited Astral Dresses, the Spirit power locked away inside Shido had completely returned to Tohka.

He remembered another time when Kotori had caused all her power to flow back to her.

When that happened, Kotori had explained that a limited amount of power flowing back to the Spirit would naturally return to him after some time, but a complete reversal would stabilize it in the Spirit, making it necessary to seal her powers once more.

This total reversal of her power meant that Tohka was currently one-hundred-percent a Spirit. That meant her Spirit signal might be detected by the AST and set off another alarm. In order to avoid that, he needed to reseal her powers as soon as possible.

"Ungh..."

However.

Sweat dripped down his cheeks.

Resealing. That, of course, meant…kissing the subject.

But everyone was injured. He couldn't go chasing them all out of the nurse's room or casually taking Tohka outside.

"Mm? What's wrong, Shido?" Tohka tilted her head to one side curiously.

His heart skipped a beat, but he waved a hand to try and shake it off. "Oh, nothing…"

And then his eye caught sight of a certain something.

Rails ran across the ceiling of the room, encircling each of the beds, and white curtains hung down from them.

This was a high school nurse's room. It was only natural that there'd be curtains to separate the beds.

"Y-you mind, gang?" he said. "I need to talk with Tohka a sec."

"…?"

The Spirits all turned curious eyes on him, but then they quickly nodded.

After getting their permission, Shido released the curtain from the wall and pulled it around Tohka's bed.

"Shido?" Tohka arched an eyebrow. "What exactly are you doing?"

"Yeah. The truth is…" He brought his face to her ear and quickly but simply explained the resealing situation.

Nodding along, Tohka suddenly grew red in the face.

And then she whirled her head around to check that there was no one listening in before turning her eyes back on him.

"Mm," she said. "So then. You mean. That. Um. You know. We do that…here?"

"Uhhh." He scratched his head. "Well, yeah, I guess that's what I mean."

"H-huh…" Tohka let her eyes roam uncertainly for a while, but eventually, she nodded firmly—like she had made up her mind—clasped her hands together in front of her chest, and closed her eyes. The perfect expression of her readiness to receive a kiss.

"Ungh." He had been the one to bring it up, but seeing Tohka like this, he froze on the spot.

She looked just like Sleeping Beauty. A beautiful sleeping form such that the utterly ordinary steel-framed bed and white curtain almost came to look like a forest of thorns.

But he couldn't simply stand here forever. He took a deep breath to calm himself before bringing his lips toward those of Tohka lying flat in the bed.

However.

"...?"

When he'd gotten his face close enough that he could feel Tohka's breath, he abruptly lifted his eyes. He couldn't help feeling that they were being watched.

"Whoa!" he cried out.

His feeling had been correct. The curtain that he'd made sure was fully closed was now open a teensy bit, and the heads of Yoshino, Yoshinon, Kaguya, Yuzuru, Miku, and Natsumi were stacked up, all their eyes staring intently at Shido and Tohka.

"Sh-Shido, what are you...?"

"Whoa! Pretty daring in a place like this, huh?"

"Oh-ho! Shido's proclivities include taking advantage of a sleeping girl?"

"Disconcertion. This is a type of necrophilia."

"Ooh, no fair only giving it to Tohka! Daaarling! Do me, too! Me toooo!"

"Y-you can't just go showing off your happy little life!"

The five girls and one puppet poured past the curtain.

"Wh-whoa!"

"Mm? Wh-what's going on?!"

Shido and Tohka were pushed up against the bed in the jostling crush.

Although Miku's Requiem had worked, the wounds of the Spirits were deep. Pressed up against one another, the pain made them all scream in the school nurse's office.

Rather than look up at the stars above the city, she looked down.

Streetlights. Lights in windows. Car headlights. The illumination colored the city. Staring down at the countless stars shining in the darkness from the roof of a tall building overlooking Tengu, Kurumi Tokisaki narrowed her eyes in a smile.

She was a beautiful girl in a dress that was red like blood and black like shadows. Her hair, which was tied up into two asymmetrical bundles, was jet-black. Her skin was white like porcelain. Each and every one of these elements was more than enough to burn her image into anyone's retinas. But the feature that lingered longest in the memories of those who came face-to-face with her was undoubtedly her distinctive eyes.

Right and left, different colors. But this was no mere case of heterochromia. Her left eye, shining with golden light, had a small clockface etched into it, and the hands of a clock marked the time. *Tick. Tick.*

Naturally, a girl with a clock for an eye could not be an ordinary human being.

She was a Spirit—a world-ending catastrophe.

That's what humanity considered Spirits to be, and she had become one of them.

"..."

She let out a short sigh.

It wasn't so much that she was especially moved by the scene spreading out below her or that she was immersing herself in sweet sentimentalism. She had long abandoned such naïveté. She didn't gladly climb up to the roofs of tall buildings because she wanted to partake in the view at night. She did it because a position that allowed her to look out over the area made it easier for her to grasp the location of the Kurumis.

It was simply that she had learned a certain something through her other selves.

"Oh my, oh my." She shrugged and sighed again.

Before some minutes had passed, she felt another presence on the supposedly deserted rooftop and whirled around.

"Well, if this isn't an odd little customer!" she said, turning her eyes to her visitor.

A girl wrapped in snowy-white dress. The clarity of her silhouette even in the middle of the night was thanks to the faint light radiating from this outfit. Without a doubt, the girl was wearing an Astral Dress just like Kurumi.

However.

The corners of Kurumi's lips curled up at the abrupt visit from this Spirit.

"It's been quite a while, Origami," she said.

Yes. The face of this Spirit was that of the former AST member and Kurumi's former classmate Origami Tobiichi.

"Hee-hee-hee!" Kurumi giggled. "It seems that I did indeed make the right choice not to take you back then. I never dreamed you'd become so truly scrumptious. You've far surpassed my expectations."

"..."

The look on Origami's face didn't change, even when Kurumi licked her lips. There was none of the previous guardedness, confusion, and even loathing in her expression.

Perhaps she intended to imply that she had no need to be on guard against Kurumi. But most likely not. Kurumi had no proof of it, but for some reason, she felt like she saw a different intent lurking deep in Origami's eyes. Something big enough that she could ignore all the other emotions this reunion inspired in her.

But she couldn't see all the way to what that intent was.

They looked at each other silently for a period, and then Kurumi sighed.

"All that said, though, it's quite the feat finding me like you did."

"..."

Origami slowly moved a hand forward. A hand that clasped the neck of a limp Kurumi.

"Ungh… Ah…"

The girl with the same face as Kurumi groaned in agony. Looking at her, Kurumi could see painful tears all over her Astral Dress. It seemed that she had a rough go of it.

"The way I am now, it's not too hard for me to catch the avatars you have spread out through the city, even if I can't immediately find you yourself," Origami said, and released the neck of the Kurumi.

"Ngh! *Cough! Cough!*"

Falling prostrate on the roof, the Kurumi coughed a few times before disappearing into the shadows as she looked up at Origami hatefully.

"My goodness!" Kurumi cooed. "Such violence."

"I held back," Origami said flatly. "I didn't kill her."

"Hmm. Is that so?" Kurumi furrowed her brow as she ran a finger over her lips. "Well then, what on earth could you want from me? You can't possibly think you can defeat me now that you've become a Spirit? If you're measuring me against the strength of my avatar, you're in for a rather painful surprise." She curled her fingers upward, as if challenging Origami to come for her.

But Origami didn't attack. She simply stared quietly at Kurumi as she said, "I didn't come to fight you."

Kurumi supposed she could believe that. If Origami had indeed come here with hostile intentions, she would have killed her avatar rather than letting her escape.

However, the corners of Kurumi's lips turned up daringly. "Goodness! Those don't sound like the words of the Spirit-hating Origami. Are you quite certain you don't want to strike me down? I *am* a Spirit, and I *have* killed any number of people, you know?"

"…"

Here, for the first time, Origami's eyebrow twitched. Even so, she did not move to attack.

Kurumi truly didn't understand what Origami was here for. She shrugged theatrically. "In that case, what is it, then? I'm assuming you're not here to invite me out for a cup of tea?"

Origami dropped her head forward with the same serious expression. "I want you to answer one question."

"A question, is it? Hee-hee-hee! Whether I am able to answer or not does depend on the content of the question, however," she said playfully.

Origami appeared to take this as a sign of consent. She stared straight at Kurumi and continued. "Your Angel, Zafkiel, manipulates time. And each of the twelve numbers on the clockface have different abilities."

"..."

Kurumi stroked her chin silently.

What Origami was saying was largely correct. But this was nothing to be especially alarmed about. Although she had no recollection of explaining her Angel, Origami had witnessed her using Zafkiel on a previous occasion.

However. Kurumi ended up unconsciously frowning at what Origami said next.

"Is one of those twelve a bullet that sends its target back to the past?" Origami asked, correctly guessing at the ability of the final, twelfth bullet, Yud Bet, the one Kurumi had yet to show anyone.

But for a girl as perceptive as Origami, it was a simple thing to infer Zafkiel's remaining abilities from the ones she had seen so far. When it came to the power to manipulate time, perhaps it was only natural that going against the current of time would come to mind.

"Even if it was, why would that matter to you?" Kurumi asked in return, a skeptical look on her face.

It would have been easy for her to lie or play innocent. But Kurumi didn't do that. She was a bit taken aback at the suddenness of it, and above all else, she felt like the moment she said it didn't have that ability, she would be somehow denying her own greatest wish.

Taking this response as an affirmation, Origami said, "Kurumi Tokisaki. I want to borrow your power."

"What?" Kurumi's eyes automatically widened at the unexpected words.

"I said I want to borrow your power," Origami repeated. "The power of your Angel."

"Dear me, dear me." Kurumi stroked her chin as she let her gaze crawl over Origami as if assessing her intentions. "Are you demanding that I use Yud Bet for your sake?"

"Yes." Origami nodded.

"..."

Kurumi produced a gentle smile and slowly opened her right hand. An old-fashioned military rifle popped out of the shadows and fell into her grasp. At the same time, she turned the barrel on Origami and pulled the trigger without hesitation.

The shadow bullet shot toward Origami.

But when it was on the verge of digging into her soft skin, her body disappeared into light. The shadow bullet lost its target and ripped through the dark night.

A moment later, Kurumi felt a presence behind her and whirled around. There stood Origami.

"Your power's vast," the Spirit in white said. "But it's meaningless if you can't hit your target."

"Goodness me! That is quite the magic trick you've learned, hmm?" Kurumi laughed cheerily to keep Origami from seeing how upset she was. "But that was my answer. Unfortunately, I simply won't be able to assist you in your aims. Yud Bet is special among the bullets I have. There's no reason why I would ever fire it for you."

Yud Bet was Kurumi's final bullet. And the sole method by which she could achieve her long-held desire. She was under no obligation to use it for Origami showing up out of nowhere or anyone else.

"..."

Origami kept staring into her eyes, motionless.

After who knew how long staring each other down like this, Kurumi sighed, defeated by Origami's persistence.

"At any rate, I shall at least ask you. For what purpose do you intend to use Yud Bet? The reason can't actually be something so trite as you wish to see an innocent Shido in his childhood, I assume?"

It wasn't that she had changed her mind. She was merely curious in what Origami wanted to do with Yud Bet now that she had attained the powers of a Spirit.

"…"

After thinking for a moment or two, Origami nodded and said, "I want you to shoot me. I want you to send me to August third, five years ago."

"Five years ago?" Kurumi frowned dubiously. "And what on earth do you intend to do then?"

Origami's gaze instantly grew harder. "I will go back in time and kill the Spirit who killed my parents. I will make it so that my mother and father never died. I will use this power to change history." She clenched her hands into fists as if to express her resolve physically.

Hearing this, Kurumi gasped slightly. "Is…that what you want?"

It wasn't that she was particularly overwhelmed by Origami's determination. It was just that for a second, she could see herself reflected in the other girl's objective.

"What do you intend to do should I refuse you?" she asked.

"Do everything possible to make you agree," Origami said immediately.

"Hmm. That's quite the sentiment." Kurumi scowled and turned the barrel of her gun on Origami once again.

She could easily see that some kind of force was included in the words *do everything possible*. She could tell Origami would try to *make* Kurumi fire Yud Bet if that mood struck her. Was she looking down on Kurumi, or was she drunk on the Spirit powers she had so abruptly obtained?

No. She found it hard to believe that *the* Origami Tobiichi would misjudge her power for such a reason. In which case, maybe she had spoken those words, so close to being a full-on challenge, because she really thought she could force Kurumi to submit. Or maybe she had come to Kurumi without having calculated anything whatsoever.

It was difficult to imagine that clever Origami would act in a way that was even remotely reckless. Still, Kurumi couldn't help feeling that the latter was the truth about Origami's presence before her now.

The reason cool and collected Origami would proceed without considering the consequences. The reason she would come to an enemy to beg for a favor she had no proof was even possible.

The possibility of redoing an incident long passed.

That sweet temptation slipped into the heart with incredible ease and ate away at it like a drug. It triggered an undeniable yearning that compelled all to seek it out, whether they realized what they were doing or not.

Kurumi understood this painfully well.

"…"

She lowered the gun. "Well, I suppose I could. Personally, I was a bit anxious about the idea of heading into the main event without having ever fired Yud Bet. I could allow you to be my lab rat."

"…! Really?" Origami said, her eyes flying open. The look on her face was impossibly straightforward for the usual Origami. She looked like an innocent child.

"You're really throwing me for a loop here." Kurumi scratched at her cheek and cleared her throat as if to regain her composure. "At any rate, the use of Yud Bet requires an immense amount of Spirit power. Naturally, I have absolutely no interest in using my own for your sake. Are you able to pay this price?"

"Yes. How much do you need?" Origami asked, her eyes serious.

Kurumi held up her index finger and touched it to her lip, as if in thought. "It varies depending on how far away the date you wish to move to is. The further back in the past, the more Spirit power is expended, and exponentially at that. So much so that to go back thirty years might effectively burn out a single Spirit's life."

"Thirty years?" Origami looked at her dubiously.

Kurumi waved a hand to dismiss the question and looked into Origami's eyes once more. "Also… Yes, there's that. The amount of Spirit power used changes according to the length of time spent at the destination. But I haven't tested this personally, so I don't have the most solid grasp on how this works. I assume naturally that you won't be returned to the present the moment you reach the past, but I may not be able to handle detailed time specifications."

"Fine. If I finish things quickly, there's no issue," Origami replied immediately.

She had an excess of confidence. Kurumi saw no uncertainty or hesitation in those eyes.

In fact, with Origami as she was now, even if she expended the Spirit power required to go back in time five years, she would have more than enough power left to fight. The concentration of Spirit power clinging to Origami was so great that Kurumi could feel it pushing up against her even just standing there with her.

"Is that so? Well, then." Kurumi turned on a heel, grabbed her skirt with her free hand, and curtsied theatrically. "Allow me the pleasure of starting the process, then. Come to me, Zaaaaaaaaafkiel!"

The face of an enormous clock appeared from the shadow between Kurumi's feet. Zafkiel. Kurumi's time-manipulating Angel.

With the rifle in her hand pointed upward, Kurumi stamped her feet as though stepping up stairs. *Bam, bam.*

Her shadow quickly expanded and grew, crawling across the roof the building to Origami's feet.

"What's this?" Origami must have realized something unusual was happening. She furrowed her brow slightly.

"Hee-hee-hee! I wonder if you might remember it."

The corners of Kurumi's lips turned up as she laughed. Origami had stepped on this shadow before at school.

The City of Devouring Time. Kurumi's ability to have her shadow extend and absorb time from all human beings who stepped into it. And this was not the wide range she usually used; this was the special version set up to concentrate the shadow as much as possible and directly absorb Spirit power from a specific target. Most likely, Origami was already feeling her power being rapidly drained away.

"If you want to give up on this, now is your last chance, dear. I am untrustworthy," Kurumi said, and grinned maliciously. "I might very well take your Spirit power and break our little promise, you know?"

But Origami looked straight ahead at her and made no move to avert her eyes. "Even so. My only choice is to cling to you."

"Is that right?"

These were unexpected words from the calculating Origami. Kurumi sighed, almost stunned, and waited until she had secured a sufficient amount of Spirit power from Origami before tightening her grip on the gun in her right hand.

She could, as she had just explained, drain all of Origami's Spirit power. Even if she didn't, she could still absorb more Spirit power than strictly necessary to fire Yud Bet.

But Kurumi did neither of those things. The reason was... Well, she didn't really know why herself.

Perhaps she simply wanted to see what kind of path this girl would take, this girl who much like herself had reached—stumbled, really—upon this particular means to an end. Or maybe she just wanted to see what end Origami would meet.

"Zafkiel. Twelfth Bullet. Yud Bet!" she shouted. The name of this final, unfired bullet, weaving its existence, its abilities.

Zafkiel creaked and squealed in a way she had never heard before, then began to emit a black light. The shock waves caused by Spirit power rolled out like lightning and crackled around the area.

Eventually, this dark lightning concentrated on a single point, the *XII* on the clockface, and a dense shadow poured out and was sucked into the barrel of the gun Kurumi held up.

The loaded weapon shuddered in her hand; the incredibly concentrated Spirit power raged inside the gun. It was almost like some invisible force was trying to keep her from firing the bullet. She felt like she was holding a power that went against God and reason, transcending the irreversible and inviolable entity that was time.

As she broke into a grin, Kurumi turned the barrel toward Origami. "Now then. Have a good trip, Origami. Time to make your dearest dream come true."

She pulled the trigger. An inky-black bullet shot forward, an arc of darkness trailing behind it through the air.

"…!"

The instant it touched Origami's chest, the bullet dug into her even as it seemed to pull her into its spinning trajectory. This twisting gradually grew more pronounced, and Origami was twisted with it. An instant later, she vanished from that space.

"Phew…"

A heartbeat later, Kurumi lowered her gun as she looked at the night wind caressing the spot where Origami Tobiichi had been standing only a second ago.

"Please do show me. How far will God permit this foolish, reckless act to try and rewrite the world?" Kurumi murmured almost to herself, relaxed her hand, and dropped the gun into the shadows.

"Ungh…"

Origami frowned. The moment Kurumi's bullet hit her, she'd felt her own body winding and distorting while her mind was ripped to pieces. There was no pain. But in its place were dizziness and nausea, like someone had grabbed her ankles and swung her around with wild abandon.

"…!"

A second later, she gasped unconsciously.

As her mind cleared, she suddenly felt an intense gravitational pull and a buoyancy, as though she was bobbing up into the sky.

Origami was, at that moment, upside down and falling through the air.

"Fwah!" She applied a little force, stopped in midair, and righted herself.

In terms of methodology, it was not so different from when she had operated a Territory with a CR unit. She issued a command in her mind and felt the space enveloping her shift and change according to her will.

Perhaps the power of Spirits and that of Wizards shared some fundamental nature. Or maybe Origami simply connected this sensation with that of the CR unit in her memory as the way to intuitively handle the Spirit power. She couldn't say for sure, but either way, it was a bit of good fortune for her.

If she hadn't already been familiar with the sensation of flying, she almost certainly would've failed to make that split-second decision and wound up slamming into the ground. That said, in her current form, a mere fall from on high wouldn't kill her.

"Where am I...?" Furrowing her brow at the dull pain lingering in her head, Origami sent her gaze racing through the air.

It was a curious sensation. The sky, which had been pitch-black until a moment ago, was now bright, like the whole scene had been rewound. She couldn't tell the exact time, but it looked to be late afternoon, the time of day when the sun was low in the sky and the building shadows began to stretch out.

When she looked around at the city from above, she realized that the scene on the ground was a bit different from the roof of the building where she'd been.

There was essentially no change in the layout of the main roads and the grid of the neighborhoods. However, the structures that populated them and the signs hung outside were different from the ones in Origami's memory.

Origami also noticed the trees along the road and in the parks were not how she remembered them. The red leaves of the trees she had been looking at were now the verdant green of midsummer.

She turned her gaze downward, looking directly below herself. She spotted a variety of heavy machinery, centered around the foundation of what would eventually become the basement of a skyscraper.

Now that she was thinking about it, Origami realized the building where she had been talking with Kurumi was still under construction five years ago.

Having confirmed all this, she lifted her face once more.

"Tengu, five years ago."

When she said the words, she felt goose bumps all over her body. Her heart pounded faster with excitement, and for a moment, she was speechless.

But that was only natural. Who on earth could blame her for the momentary lapse when she realized that her utterly unattainable dream was finally within reach? Five years ago. And who on earth would laugh at the deep emotion of the girl who'd devoted over a quarter of her life to revenge?

She had become a Spirit and returned to the past to kill a Spirit by using the power of a Spirit. An extraordinary situation that was almost impossible to believe. A preposterous series of events that Origami most likely would have taken as nothing more than a bad joke had someone told her about it just a day earlier.

But the world that she perceived with all her senses was reality, all of it. She didn't need to pinch herself; she was certain that this was real.

Origami had come back.

August 3, five years earlier. The day her parents had been killed by the Spirit. The day she'd sought, wanted, yearned for, and yet could never reach—she had returned.

"Aah." She let out a cry of appreciation that no one would hear and exhaled softly. Then she clenched her hands into fists and sharpened her gaze, as if dedicating herself anew.

That was enough for now. Any other words would have to wait until after she had achieved her objective.

She had only just stepped onto the stage. The important part lay ahead. In her mind, Origami replayed the scene she'd witnessed that day.

The town in flames. Her parents incinerated by a light that shot down from the sky. The silhouette of the loathsome Spirit hanging above.

She would kill that Spirit before they killed her parents. She would make it so the death of her parents never happened. She would remake the world where they were dead.

She would not allow herself to shed a tear until her work was done.

Her enemies were a Spirit and the world. But there was no hint of fear or hesitation in her heart. There was nothing but a burning desire for revenge and the brilliant light of hope.

She rubbed at the corners of her eyes with a thumb as if to wipe away whatever might have welled up, turned around, and called out, "Metatron. Mal'akh."

Particles of light began to sparkle in the air around her and then concentrated on her back to manifest Metatron in the shape of wings.

She flapped the Angel wings and flew off at top speed, gliding through the sky.

Naturally, she headed south. This was the direction of Tengu's Nanko district, where she had lived until five years earlier.

Although she'd succeeded in going back in time, she had no idea exactly how long she'd be able to stay here. In which case, she had to act quickly. She wouldn't be able to bear it if she came all this way only to be unable to find the Spirit—or worse, reach the time limit before she managed to destroy the Spirit when she did find them.

Honing the murderous rage she'd carried in her heart for these many years, Origami hurried to her destination.

Before long, she heard an earsplitting noise. For a second, she thought it was the spacequake alarm, but no. It was a fire alarm. Mixed in with the sound of fire-truck and ambulance sirens.

"…!"

At the same time, Origami saw a shimmering mirage up ahead.

The town was on fire.

This was no metaphor, no joke. The residential area filling her field of vision was burning a bright red as if it had been bombed. Together with the sound of the alarm and the sirens came the crumbling of buildings, the roaring of flames, and the screams of people fleeing in confusion—a hellish scene.

Origami remembered this, too. The blaze in the Nanko district five years ago was impossibly unfolding right now before her own eyes.

"…! So then…" Calling up her memories of the past, Origami was on edge again after her brief moment of peace.

Kotori Itsuka—Spirit of fire, Efreet—had caused this blaze. When she was unable to completely control her new abilities, the aftershocks of her vast Spirit power had turned the area into a sea of flames.

In which case, *they* would be present. The *other* Spirit that had turned Kotori Itsuka into a Spirit.

"Heh!"

At the same time as Origami realized this, she decelerated and flew around the neighborhood. Sparks flew, and black smoke drifted up, making visibility extremely poor. Paying it no heed, she scanned the town below.

And then she found them. An elementary school boy and a little girl in a faintly shining Astral Dress.

"… Shido!" she cried out automatically.

Yes, it was without a doubt Origami's love, Shido Itsuka, and his little sister, Kotori Itsuka, of five years earlier.

Which meant…

"…"

Swallowing hard, she shifted her gaze slightly away from Shido and Kotori sitting on the ground.

There.

They were there.

Origami didn't know a single thing about them—age, sex, appearance—but she was certain that they were the something she had just spotted.

The Spirit that seemed to be veiled by a layer of static was standing beside the children. They did indeed strongly resemble the being that had given Origami her own Spirit powers. Were they actually the very same being?

But for Origami in that moment, this was nothing more than a mere triviality, not worth pondering.

"I…found you," she murmured.

At the same time, she felt her body temperature drop precipitously.

"I found you. Found you. Found you found you found you found you found you found you found you found you found you found you found you found you found you found you found you found you. I finally found you."

Her mind grew clear, and the only thing she could see in her field of vision was that Spirit—Phantom.

Despite the fact that Origami had at last found the target of her revenge, the very being she had longed for like an infatuated school-girl, she was extremely coolheaded. So cool that it almost felt like she had frozen over.

She was overcome with the sensation that everything about her had been optimized for killing *that*. In that moment, she was murder itself, a blade.

"Metatron," she called, raising her right hand.

The wings that had manifested on her back split into independent parts, danced up into the air, and turned their tips downward.

Beams of light shot forth from those shards of Metatron, all aimed squarely at Phantom.

But a heartbeat before the light struck home, Phantom shimmered and disappeared.

"…"

Origami didn't panic. She slowly turned her head upward and found that Phantom was now in the air, at the same altitude as her. In the blink of an eye, they had evaded Origami's attack and flown up to her.

"What's this?" Phantom said in a voice that was hard to understand. "I wondered exactly who would come and attack me from out of nowhere. You're a Spirit?"

Because of the static obscuring their body, Origami couldn't discern the finer details of their facial expression, but she could guess more or less from Phantom's bearing that they were surprised. They looked Origami over with great interest.

"And that Angel… Metatron? What exactly is this, then? I still have that Sefirah," Phantom said, cocking their head curiously to one side.

Origami was able to infer from these words that the Spirit in front of her now and the entity that had given her Spirit powers were indeed one and the same.

However, she no longer loathed herself for the fact that she had received this power from her enemy. In fact, she felt exultation, almost like superiority at this blunder on Phantom's part. The Spirit would be struck down by the very power they had given away.

"Say, who are you? Where exactly did you come from? Why did you attack me?"

"Aaaaaaaah!" Origami cried out, rather than respond, and pushed her right hand forward.

Metatron turned its tips in the same direction and fired beams of light at Phantom.

The other Spirit wriggled as they had before and dodged the attack by a hair.

"No mistake, that's Metatron. In which case, all I can think of is... Did you travel back in time with the power of Zafkiel? If you did, well...it's a bit unexpected. To think that girl would lend anyone her power," Phantom said, mostly talking to themselves. But that had nothing to do with Origami.

"Kadour!" She threw her arms open wide.

The wing-shaped Metatron fell to pieces, redeployed in the sky, and turned toward Phantom.

"Haaaaaaah!" Origami shouted, and Metatron launched another blinding attack on Phantom.

"...!"

Phantom gasped and slid through the air, barely avoiding the beams shooting toward them.

But Metatron's rush continued ceaselessly from all directions. With the first blow, Origami had been careful to hold back so as not to accidentally hurt Shido, but this attack contained her full strength.

Phantom had apparently concluded that the attacks would only continue if they remained here. The Spirit pulled back to the rear, slipping in between the Metatron blasts, and flew off into the sky as if to escape Origami.

"You're not getting away!" Origami sharpened her gaze, and with Metatron still deployed around her, she kicked at the air and went after Phantom.

Phantom traced a complicated trajectory through the air, dancing and weaving. Origami gave chase and fired shot after shot. While Phantom did manage to dodge these blows, the range of their movement was shrinking.

"Haah... It seems that future me has done something to earn quite the serious grudge," Phantom said, annoyed, as they flew around every which way, evading the beams of light in this endless game of tag. "But unfortunately for you, I can't exactly let you kill me here and now. I also have a dream that must be fulfilled."

"...!" Origami scowled. "A dream?"

Metatron danced through the air like a falcon, drawing out a line of light in the sky.

"A dream that killed...my mother...my father?" she demanded. "Absurd. No. Shut your mouth. I won't give you even a moment to dream. I won't give you a moment to pray. You will die without achieving anything. You will disappear and leave nothing behind. Vanish from this world with only regret in that void of a heart!"

Phantom cocked their head curiously to one side at Origami's words. "Your mother and father? What are you talking about? I haven't a clue. Sorry, but maybe you've got the wrong person?"

"...!"

Origami gasped.

Phantom's response was actually quite natural. At this point in time, they *hadn't* killed Origami's parents yet. Pursued for a crime they hadn't committed, the fact was there was no way they could answer for that crime.

But Phantom's response also revealed another simple fact.

Phantom had said, *"I haven't a clue."*

In other words, unless they were feigning ignorance, they weren't even aware of the names of Origami's parents or even their general existence, despite the fact that they would be killed in a few minutes had Origami not shown up.

The act had no calculation, no logic, no reason.

For this Spirit, killing Origami's parents was not because of a matter of principle or a part of some greater objective, but a whim of the moment, an incident not worth thinking about, nothing more than stepping on ants on the road.

Already dizzy with indignation, Origami felt her head spin even more wildly. Rage coursed through her body, threatening to burst out from her skin.

She herself no longer had the words to describe this sensation. Wrath. Murder. Loathing. But these could only express a fraction of the mad feelings filling her heart.

The only thing that was certain was that Phantom could absolutely not be permitted to exist in this world.

"Monsterrr!" With a scream, she attacked. Pieces of Metatron scattered throughout the sky and fired pillars of light. But Phantom managed to dodge them all with exquisite precision.

However, Origami had factored this nimble evasion into her strategy. As she deliberately fired shots that were easier to avoid, she studied Phantom's movement patterns and saw through them.

She had created a safety zone that Phantom was able to slip into. A spot where they barely managed to dodge the dangerous beams of light. In essence, this was the formation of a cage of light.

It would only hold its shape for a mere instant. But that would be plenty of time.

"Haah!"

While the beams of light still lingered in the air, Origami marshaled Metatron to form a crown above Phantom's head and used it to fire the ultimate beam of light straight downward to knock Phantom out of the sky.

"...!"

Phantom seemed dismayed for the first time.

But it was too soon to judge. Origami was sure they wouldn't get away unscathed with an attack like this.

Phantom bumped up against the cage of light and dodged by a hairbreadth, evading the dazzling pillar plummeting from above. The concentrated force of Origami's Spirit power lost its target and plunged toward the earth.

At the same time, the wall of Spirit power around Phantom and the cage of Metatron's light came into contact, sending Spirit power scattering like sparks. An intense flash lit up the area, dazzling Origami's eyes for a second.

But Phantom didn't take advantage of that opening to try and counterattack. They remained still and spoke quietly. "Quite magnificent. I indeed couldn't completely avoid that blow. I never dreamed you would wield such mastery of Metatron."

"…?"

Origami unconsciously frowned.

A second ago, she hadn't been able to tell whether Phantom's voice was masculine or feminine and could barely make out the words they were speaking. But that voice was now surprisingly clear as it hit her ears.

It was the voice of a young woman.

"But you've got me in a bit of bind, hmm? If possible, I'd like to avoid any messiness. Though, it's honestly unthinkable that I would ever pass up the chance to hand a Sefirah to a girl who can wield this much power…and that means creating a rebellious Spirit, all the while knowing that she would raise her hand against me," Phantom mused, and whirled around to turn her back to Origami.

She was not the unfathomable being blotted out by static, but rather a girl with long hair blowing in the wind.

Most likely, when she'd forcibly broken out of Origami's cage of light, the film of static that'd covered her had been temporarily disabled. Phantom's true form, unknowable to Origami before, was now exposed to the light of day.

But that was not the sole reason that Origami stayed her hand, albeit only for a few minutes. She felt like Phantom's voice was familiar somehow.

"Who are you...?"

The girl ignored Origami's question.

"Well, I suppose that doesn't really matter. The birth of a powerful Spirit should be celebrated, after all. So I will resign myself to my fate and accept this blow. All for the sake of my dream," she said, her eyes on Origami's face, and waved her hand. "Bye now. I'll be on my way. I achieved my objective here today, at any rate. The truth is, I would like to see a little more of your power, but...it doesn't look like anything good will come from staying in this place any longer."

The girl vanished slowly into the empty air.

"...! Stop!" Origami disassembled Metatron into parts once more and shot several beams of light to try and pierce the girl's back.

But she was too late.

Metatron's attack passed through the girl's shadow and stretched out into the distant sky.

"Ngh!" Origami glared at the spot in the air where Phantom had disappeared and gritted her teeth in vexation.

Regret filled every fiber of her being; she'd let the Spirit who killed her parents get away.

"..."

No. Origami shook her head as if to reject her own thought.

Phantom had indeed escaped her. She hadn't been able to get revenge for her parents. But she had achieved her most important objective.

The fact that Phantom had disappeared meant that the Spirit who would kill Origami's parents was no more.

"Ah. Ahhh," she said, throwing her head back.

Her parents didn't have to die.

This changed everything.

The world *could* be remade.

When the time limit for Kurumi's bullet ran out and she was returned to the present, the gentle smiles of her mother and father would be waiting for her.

"Mom… Dad…" Tears welled up in the corners of her eyes.

She had done it.

With her very own hands, she had gotten her parents back. A truth that supposedly could never be overturned had vanished.

And then.

"…?"

She realized something.

"This is…," she said as she looked down at the scene below her.

It wasn't particularly surprising that one part of the residential area was engulfed in flames. But when she looked more closely, she felt like she knew the shape of that street. It was the place where she had once lived.

"What?" she cried out quietly.

Directly below her was a girl. And when she saw her, Origami was overcome with the sensation of her entire body constricting.

The girl was in maybe grade five or six, with hair long enough to skim her shoulders and a hairpin to hold it in place. She had a sweet face, but it was tragically adorned with soot and a stunned expression.

"That's…" Origami spoke through trembling lips.

There was no mistake. There *could be* no mistake.

She was looking at herself from five years earlier.

"Huh… Ah."

Thump. Thump. Her heart thudded heavily in her chest. Her head spun wildly out of control.

Eyes, ears, nose. She had the overwhelming urge to block all her sensory organs, to shut out all information from the outside world.

But she had seen it.

Half-automatically, her gaze shifted.

Just beyond the elementary school version of herself collapsed on the ground.

"Ah… Ah…"

Right in front of Origami from five years ago, she caught sight of damage conspicuously greater than anything in the surrounding area.

The asphalt road was completely ripped apart. No matter how terrifying the blaze, fire wouldn't do that.

It looked almost like a beam of light had shot down from the heavens.

And scattered in the center of that crater were hunks of flesh and bone that had most likely been people a few moments earlier.

Yes. Directly below the beam of light Origami had only just fired at Phantom.

"Ah. Ah. Ah. Ah. Ah. Ah…"

Her vision swam. Her throat grew tight. Her fingertips trembled.

She had a vivid flashback to the scene she had once witnessed.

Five years earlier, returning to the neighborhood engulfed in flames, Origami had been reunited with her parents in front of their house. Her mother and father were safe. She had been profoundly relieved and delighted to see them. But in the next instant, light poured down from the sky, and her parents, who'd been standing in front of her, vanished in an instant.

A scene out of a nightmare that she could still see like it had happened yesterday, even now when she closed her eyes.

And in that moment, Origami stared up at the sky. Her gaze went to the source of the light. As if searching for the murderer who had killed her parents.

And then she'd seen it.

In the sky. A single silhouette.

Not yet knowing of the existence of the Spirits five years ago, Origami's description of what she saw was simple.

An angel.

"…"

The Origami of five years ago lifted her face and looked at the Origami of now.

As if following the girl's gaze, Origami's eyes dropped to her trembling hands. She let her eyes crawl all over her body.

A snowy-white Astral Dress covering her slender frame and giving off a faint glow. Countless "feathers" dancing in the air as if to cover her.

If someone who knew nothing about the truth saw her, she would no doubt have looked like an angel to them.

"Ah. Ah. Ah. Aaaaaaaaaaaaah!"

Her whole body shook.

Origami twisted and writhed, cradling her head in her hands.

She felt like she might be obliterated and disappear. Or maybe this was something closer to desire.

A self-loathing, a wish to erase herself right that very second, filled her skull. A despair that could not tolerate her own existence flooded the cracks in her heart.

Despair and rage bled onto the face of the little Origami on the ground, and she opened her mouth. Her voice was drowned out by the sounds of the sirens and the buildings collapsing, so Origami couldn't hear it.

But she didn't need that voice to reach her ears; the words rang clearly in her head.

You...

You won't get away with this! I'll kill you... I swear I'll kill you! That's a promise...!

That.

It was the very curse that Origami had replayed over and over in her mind.

She understood everything now.

She knew.

Five years ago. Just as Shido said, there had indeed been multiple Spirits in the bonfire of Tengu's Nanko district. But there hadn't been *two* Spirits. There had been three.

Kotori Itsuka—Efreet—who had caused the fire.

Phantom, the one who had turned Kotori into a Spirit.

And the one who had come from the future to strike down Phantom, Origami.

"I…killed…Mom and Dad?" she said hoarsely.

Yes. Phantom had not killed her parents.
The blast that had killed her parents was none other than the light of Metatron fired by Origami herself.
"Ah. Ah. Ah."
The moment she realized this, Origami felt like the colors of the scene unfolding before her inverted.
"Aaaaaaaaaaaaaaaaaaaaaaaaaaaaaaaaaaaaaaaaaaaaaaaaaaaaaaaaaa
aaaaaaaaaaaaaaaaaaaaaaaaaaaaaaaaaaaaaaaaaaaaaaaaaaaaaaaaaaaa
aaaaaaaaaaaaaaaaaaaaaaaaaaaaaaaaaaaaaaaaaaaaaaaaaaaaaaaaaaaa
aaaaaaaaaaaaaaaaaaaaaaaaaaaaaaaaaaaaaaaaaaaaaaaaaaaaaaaaaaaa
aaaaaaaaaaaaaaaaaaaaaaaaaaaaaaaaaaaaaaaaaaaaaaaaaaaaaaaaaaaa
aaaaaaaaaaaaaaaaaaaaaaaaaaaaaaaaaaaaaaaaaaaaaaaaaaaaaaaaaaaa
aaaaaaaaaaaaaaaaaaaaaaaaaaaaaaaaaaaaaaaaaaaaaaaaaaaaaaaaaaaa
aaaaaaaaaaaaaaaaaaaaaaaaaaaaaaaaaaaaaaaaaaaaaaaaaaaaaaaaaaaa
aaaaaaaaaaaaaaaaaaaaaaaaaaaaaaaaaaaaaaaaaaaaaaaaaaaaaaaaaaaa
aaaaaaaaaaaaaaaaaaaaaaaaaaaaaaaaaaaaaaaaaaaaaaaaaaaaaaaaaaaa
aaaaaaaaaaaaaaaaaaaaaaaaaaaaaaaaaaaaaaaaaaaaaaaaaaaaaaaaaaaa
aaaaaaaaaaaaaaaaaaaaaaaaaaaaaaaaaaaaaaaaaaaaaaaaaaaaaaaaaaaa
aaaaaaaaaaaaaaaaaaaaaaaaaaaaaaaaaaaaaaaaaaaaaaaaaaaaaaaaaaaa
aaaaaaaaaaaaaaaaaaaaaaaaaaaaaaaaaaaaaaaaaaaaaaaaaaaaaaaaaaaa
aaaaaaaaaaaaaaaaaaaaaaaaaaaaaaaaaaaaaaaaaaaaaaaaaaaaaaaaaaaa
aaaaaaaaaaaaaaaaaaaaaaaaaaaaaaaaaaaaaaaaaaaaaaaaaaaaaaaaaaaa
aaaaaaaaaaaaaaaaaaaaaaaaaaaaaaaaaaaaaaaaaaaaaaaaaaaaaaaaaaah!"
It was like her world had turned inside out.
Just as her mind was on the verge of unconsciousness, Origami felt her heart turn inky black.

Chapter 5
Demon King of Descending Darkness

The time was ten thirty PM. Shido and the girls were in a room in a hospital in the city.

The spacequake alarm had been called off before too long, and the people returned to the town and school. The health teacher found them locked away in the nurse's room with grave injuries and demanded to know why they hadn't evacuated. After giving them a good scolding, she immediately sent them to the hospital.

Although they were in a sealed state, the Spirits were still much hardier than any human being. Their wounds also healed much, much faster.

Even so, given that none of them could heal their wounds on the spot like Kotori or Kurumi, the girls were very obviously worse for the wear. It was only natural that the health teacher had dialed 119, brooking no argument. But Shido had wanted to take them to the hospital from the start, so this development actually saved him some work.

"Mm. Shido, I'm hungry," Tohka said, neatly bandaged up.

Flashing a weary smile, he shrugged. They'd only just had supper a little while ago, but clearly, the standard hospital meal was not enough for her.

"Honestly. Well, if you're hungry, you're hungry. But it's late, so it's gotta be something light. How about I go pick up some jelly at the store?"

"Mm!" Tohka nodded energetically.

Watching this exchange from the side, the other Spirits pursed their lips and voiced their displeasure.

"Come now, Shido. What manner of behavior is this, to give our retainer the forbidden fruit whilst pushing us to the side?"

"Dissatisfaction. You lack the proper awareness for a piece of property shared by Yuzuru and Kaguya."

"Aaaah. No fair always asking Tohka!"

Fortunately, a whole large room had been empty, and so they'd all been able to stick together. Shido, Yoshino, and Natsumi hadn't been hurt really, but because they no longer had a home to go back to, they were allowed to stay at the hospital with the girls until space in a shelter opened up.

There were several temporary facilities that could take in residents who'd lost their dwellings to Spirit damage in Tengu. But this time, the destruction had mostly hit residential neighborhoods and more people than usual had lost their homes, and it would be a while before the system could get them all a place to stay.

The disastrous scene around the Itsuka house was explained away as spacequake damage. But that made sense. Origami had likely acted with that intention all along. To start with, what was generally referred to as spacequake damage was actually the explosion when a Spirit manifested in this world, combined with the aftermath from the battle between the Spirit and AST. This was definitely not a significant deviation from that definition.

"Yeah, yeah. I'll get something for everyone. Just hang on. Yoshino? Natsumi? You want something, too?" he asked, looking toward the far end of the room.

Yoshino and Natsumi sat together on folding chairs there. Actually, to be more precise, the two of them had their eyes closed and were snoozing, leaning against each other. It seemed that they had fallen asleep, exhausted.

"Ha-ha-ha!" His expression softened as he grabbed one of the extra blankets and covered them with it. A lot had happened that day. He wasn't surprised they were tired.

"Hmm?" He furrowed his brow slightly. He could hear a vibrating sound coming from somewhere.

"Mm. What's wrong, Shido?" Tohka asked.

"Oh, some kind of weird noise... Ah!" He realized what the source of the sound was—the vibration of a cell phone.

"Maybe Yoshino's? Now that I'm thinking about it, I forgot to get her to turn it off before we came into the hospital." Shido groaned as he scratched his cheek. Cell phones were, of course, completely taboo in the hospital, but it was harsh to expect the Spirits to know this. It was his mistake for forgetting to warn her.

"Welp, I can't just let it ring like that." He didn't know who the call was from, but it would only make things worse if he let it ring and they called again. He reached a hand out to Yoshino's pocket to turn the phone off.

"Huh?"

But the phone he was after was not in that pocket. Maybe she had put it somewhere else. He searched the girl, following the vibrations of the call.

"Oh! Found it." He discovered the phone in a pocket farther back and reached for it.

"Mm... Unnn..." Yoshino moaned like something was tickling her and slowly opened her eyes. After looking around dazed for a moment or two, she saw Shido's face in front of her and his hand moving around groping her, and her face turned deep red.

"...! Ah. Um... Shido...?!" she said, and froze in place, tears springing up in the corners of her eyes.

Shido suspected there had been an obvious misunderstanding. "Th-this isn't what it looks like, Yoshino! This— Okay, it's just..."

"Mm... What's all the fuss...? Wah. Uh..." Waking up next to Yoshino, Natsumi opened her eyes wide, raised her right hand, and landed a magnificent uppercut on Shido's jaw. "You filthy bruuuuuuuute!"

"Hampf?!" Shido let out an indecipherable cry as he was sent flying by the force of Natsumi's punch, slamming into the floor of the hospital room on his back.

Ding, ding, ding! The gong to signal the end of a fight rang. That's what it felt like to him, at least.

"Sh-Shido?!" Tohka cried out in surprise.

Because Yoshino and Natsumi were sitting exactly on the other side of the curtain, it was in a blind spot from the perspective of the girls in the beds. To Tohka and the other Spirits, it looked as though Shido had abruptly fallen over.

He waved a hand weakly to indicate that he was okay and slowly pulled himself upright, rubbing his chin.

"A-are you okay, Yoshino?!" Natsumi demanded. "That monkey didn't do anything weird to you, did he?!"

"Uh. Um. Y-yes. But Shido…"

"Just forget about that jerk! I—I can't believe he'd try something so shameless when I was sleeping right beside you!"

"I-it's a misunderstanding. I was only—" Shido tried to present Yoshino's cell phone, still clutched in his hand, as evidence in his case. But there, he stopped and furrowed his brow.

The reason was simple. A familiar name was displayed on the screen of Yoshino's phone.

"…!"

He immediately tapped the ANSWER button and pressed the phone to his ear. He was only too aware that talking on cell phones was prohibited in the hospital, but his body acted on instinct before his brain had the chance to process it.

"*…Hello? Yoshino?*"

He heard a familiar voice over the speaker.

"Kotori?! Is that you?" he replied, excited.

Yes. The voice he heard was without a doubt that of his own little sister, Kotori.

"Mm?!"

"Oh-ho! So she is well after all?"

As if in reaction to the name Shido cried out, Tohka and the other Spirits raised their voices. Shido nodded at them and then returned his focus to the phone.

"*Shido? Phew. That's a relief. So you're all right? What about everyone else?*"

"They're good. Well, I can't quite say that, but at any rate, they're alive."

"*Yeah? That's what's important anyway.*"

"So, like, I should be asking you the same thing," he said. "Where are you? Is *Fraxinus* okay? We kept trying to call and couldn't get through. I was worried."

Kotori fell silent. All he could hear was a somehow chagrined inhalation and exhalation.

"Kotori...?"

"*I'm in one of Ratatoskr's underground facilities,*" she said finally. "*The crew's all more or less okay. But...we lost. It was a total defeat.*"

"Huh?!" His eyes flew open in surprise at this unexpected declaration. "Wh-what do you mean?"

"*Exactly what I said. We got done in by DEM. Cumulative damage of over thirty percent to the entire ship. It was all we could do to use up Yggdrafolium and get out of there.* Fraxinus *is being repaired. We barely managed to protect the airship with the Territory. But assume it'll be out of operation for the time being.*"

Shido was at a loss for words. It wasn't that he didn't understand what she was saying. But the image of *Fraxinus* and the word *defeat* were refusing to connect properly in his brain.

When he actually thought about it, though, it wasn't unthinkable. *Fraxinus* was an airship. And this sort of thing happened. He had simply assumed that absolute safety was guaranteed aboard *Fraxinus*.

"*Fraxinus*?! But I thought the Ratatoskr Realizers outperformed DEM's...?" he said.

"*As a general rule, yes,*" Kotori replied. "*But ever since DEM developed its new Ashcroft-beta model, the gap's closed a whole lot. And DEM has that woman.*"

"…!"

That woman. The instant Shido heard those words, the face of that woman popped up in his mind. Silky, pale-gold hair, blue eyes brimming with self-confidence. The face of the most powerful Wizard, Ellen Mathers.

In that silence, Kotori understood that Shido had grasped the situation. She let out a sigh before continuing.

"*Well, what's done is done, though. Anyway, tell me. Where on earth did you disappear to? And you said everyone's alive. That mean they took down Origami Tobiichi?*"

"Oh, the thing is…," he mumbled, sighed, and then briefly explained the events of a few hours earlier.

How Origami locked him up. How he was rescued by Yoshino and Natsumi. And how when he raced to the Spirits' battlefield, he saw Origami, transformed into a Spirit.

"*Origami Tobiichi is a Spirit?!*" Kotori cried, stunned. "*Meaning? You're saying Phantom showed up?*"

"I don't know," he said. "But that's the only thing I can think of."

"*…! What the? Why at a time like this?!*" Kotori said angrily. But that was no wonder at all. She had a deep, fateful connection with Phantom. "*So then where's Origami Tobiichi?*"

"She flew off somewhere. I've got no idea where she went."

"*Uh-huh. Got it. We'll try tracking her down on our end. Shido, you just prepare yourself.*"

He frowned. "Prepare myself?"

"*Well, yeah. Whoever she might be, a Spirit's a Spirit. We'll have to target Origami Tobiichi next, y'know?*"

"Oh…"

Now that she mentioned it, that was exactly right. Shido's role was to raise his likability with the Spirit, kiss her, and seal her Spirit powers. Naturally, Origami would be no exception.

But somehow, when he thought about it being Origami, he couldn't help but picture Origami preying on him rather than the usual mission. It might have been essential for sealing her power, but he felt like there would be real consequences if he kissed her.

Perhaps guessing at Shido's train of thought, Kotori sighed. *"Well, there's still a bunch of questions I'd like to ask you, but let's leave all that for when we meet up again. I don't want to keep you on the phone too long in the hospital."*

"Huh?" He was surprised. "How do you know…?"

"Whose phone are you talking on right now, hmm?"

"Ohhh. Right." Shido nodded. Now that she mentioned it, he felt like he'd heard something about a transmitter being embedded in the phones provided to the Spirits, in case of emergency.

"I sent some people out to come get you. They should be there soon. Just follow their instructions. We'll talk to the hospital. You just make sure you're ready to leave."

"Okay, got it. But everyone's hurt…"

"Don't worry. This place isn't quite up to Fraxinus *standards, but we've at least got medical Realizers here. The girls'll heal faster here than lying there in a regular hospital."*

"I guess that makes sense. Got it." Shido glanced around the room, looking at each of the Spirits in turn, and sighed. Fortunately, none of them were so badly injured that they'd have any trouble moving on their own.

"My staff should be arriving now. We'll talk details later."

As Kotori said this, he heard the sound of engines outside.

He stood up and looked at the window to find several vehicles that were not ambulances parked beside the hospital. This had to be the staff Kotori was talking about.

Shido realized that it had gotten quite dark. The sky had long turned black, and the perfect circle of a moon shone brightly.

"Aah, okay. Talk to you later." He said good-bye and was about to hang up.

"Nice work, Ellen."

A voice called out to Ellen as she stepped inside her hotel room, having succeeded magnificently at her mission and finished up a number of tasks.

When she looked over, she found Isaac Westcott sitting on the sofa, apparently awaiting her to return.

"Ike," she greeted him.

"That was truly a wonderful performance," he said. "I'd expect nothing less of you."

"No, being hit even once was a miscalculation," Ellen responded. "The enemy seems to have an excellent crew."

Westcott chuckled as he shrugged. "So then is that crew safe and sound?"

"That's unclear. I did urge them to evacuate, but that suggestion was refused."

"Was it, then? That's unfortunate. I do hope that as many of them as possible survived," Westcott said with no hint of sarcasm. He was, in fact, serious. Ellen's target had been Ratatoskr's airship, not its crew. The ship itself, with its ability to interfere with DEM's activities, was a thorn in his side. It suited his ends quite well, however, to leave them with enough strength to protect the Spirits and place them with Shido Itsuka.

That said, however, not every member of Ratatoskr was stuffed into that ship. Even if, hypothetically, the crew had been wiped out, that man—Woodman—would find a way to expertly fill those vacancies.

Westcott was well aware of this fact. In contrast with his words, no hint of gloom could be seen on his face.

"More importantly, Ike..." Ellen said.

"Yes, I know." Westcott dipped his head forward as if to say that he agreed before turning the terminal on the table toward Ellen.

An image was displayed on the screen. The figure of Origami Tobiichi clad in a snowy-white Astral Dress.

Ellen had also detected the appearance of a new Spirit signal on the ground with the measurement devices aboard her ship. But she had indeed doubted her ears when she heard the report from head office.

Because in the middle of a battle against the Spirits, Origami Tobiichi had become a Spirit.

"Ha-ha! This truly was unexpected, hmm? To think that she would turn into a Spirit!" Westcott broke into a great big smile, like this was the most amusing thing to happen yet. "Wait. Perhaps I should lament the loss of an excellent Wizard. Aah, how dreadful. That said, I'm sure she'll be an asset to us."

"You're smiling, Ike."

"Whoopsy! Excuse me." Even as he said this, Westcott did not bother to cover his mouth.

Ellen sighed before continuing. "So then where is she now?"

"Oh, yes. She was apparently flying around Tengu until earlier, but then her signal abruptly disappeared."

"It disappeared? Do you suppose this means she has the ability to mask her power?"

"You think so, too?" Westcott asked.

"If she's a Spirit, it's obvious that we'll target her," Ellen replied. "It's only natural that she would hide."

"I wonder about that. It's certainly a reasonable conclusion to reach, but a Spirit is a Spirit precisely because they are beyond the realm of what we can imagine." As he spoke, Westcott stood up from the sofa and walked leisurely toward the window.

Outside, a cloudless night sky spread out, with the moon enshrined precisely in the center of it.

"Who knows? She might be watching us from right over there," he said jokingly, a smile stretching across his lips.

"Did Origami manage to complete her objective, then?" Kurumi said, as though speaking to herself, sitting on the edge of a building rooftop beneath the moonlit sky. "Hee-hee-hee! I do wonder."

"Most likely, she couldn't." A voice that was the same as hers came from the shadows. "The world is strong. The dream of one little girl won't shatter it so easily."

"Oh goodness!" another voice declared. "I don't know. Have you seen Origami? With that much power, it's certainly possible."

"And what do *I* think, then?"

One after another, her chatty avatars spoke up.

Kurumi sighed and shrugged, her skinny shoulders bobbing up and down. "I can't say anything, really. If I were to voice my personal hope, though, I would say that I sincerely wish Origami success in fulfilling her dream."

Her shadow avatars giggled.

"Hee-hee-hee! I'm surprised to hear that from me. Is the light of the moon perhaps having an effect on you?"

How inexcusably rude.

But rather than getting angry at her avatar, Kurumi curled her lips into a smile and stared up at the magnificent moon hanging in the sky.

Some might say the light of the moon drives people mad. If that were true, then it might well have been that the moon had been the reason for a certain lunatic whim of Kurumi's that night.

"Well, that's all right, isn't it? That sort of mood strikes from time to time, no?" she said, putting her weight onto her hands and getting ready to do a nimble backflip.

And then the moon hanging in the sky split in two.

"Huh?" Looking up at the sky from the hospital room, Shido opened his eyes wide in surprise.

A crack raced down across the moon in a straight line. Naturally, the moon couldn't actually split apart. He quickly realized it was merely a shadow on the face of the brightly shining satellite.

But what he didn't know was where that shadow was coming from. It wasn't a cloud, some kind of bird, or an airplane. The moon had been neatly severed in two, almost like a rupture in space itself.

"What? Something going on?"

He heard Kotori's dubious voice over the phone pressed to his ear. But Shido couldn't answer her.

He watched as the rupture steadily ate into the moon to black out its light, almost like an eclipse.

It was then that he noticed it wasn't just the moon.

"What the…?"

This rupture of darkness was filling in the already-dark night sky.

He strained his eyes to look harder at what was going on and finally understood. Beneath the dark sky, an even inkier darkness was weaving a spider's web.

At first glance, he couldn't tell exactly how wide a range it covered. All the sky that he could see was being invaded by this darkness. It might have been the neighborhood, or the whole city, or the whole of the Kanto region, or…

It grew and grew, making him picture greater and greater areas. A darkness different from the night filling the sky.

The web of darkness squirmed like a living creature, and their hospital room shuddered violently.

"Wha—?!"

"Ngh!"

"E-earthquake?!"

"Eeeek!"

Panicking, the Spirits clung to the curtain or tried to hide under the bed.

But Shido instinctively felt that this shaking was no regular earthquake.

As if to back up his hunch, another phenomenon he doubted was natural struck the hospital room. Something that could only be described as a black beam of light, of concentrated darkness, poured down from the sky, shot through the ceiling and floor, and passed down to the floors below.

A few moments later, it hit the ground. An even more intense shock rocked the hospital room.

"Ah!" he cried. "Wh-what is this?!"

For a second, he thought maybe a DEM Wizard had shown up overhead and was taking shots at him and the Spirits. But that wasn't it.

When he looked out the window, he saw streams of darkness pouring down.

"Wha—?"

The sight left him speechless.

The black beams were constant and merciless, easily piercing the buildings on the ground, destroying them in the blink of an eye. Trees were mowed down, cars exploded, the roads shattered. The quiet neighborhood was destroyed in an instant, transformed into a hellish scene of pandemonium.

"Wh-what's happening, Shido?!" Tohka jumped out of bed in a panic.

A shrill alarm began ringing, loud enough to be heard in every part of the city.

At the same time, he heard a siren over the phone, the line he still had open to Kotori. It sounded slightly different from the alarm on *Fraxinus*, but there was no mistaking it. This was the sound to mark the appearance of a Spirit.

"…! Kotori, this is—"

"*A Spirit! But the way it's manifesting…!*" Kotori sounded just as shocked as he felt. "*This powerful of a Spirit appearing without any warning whatsoever… It's…*"

"…?"

He furrowed his brow when Kotori slowed to a stop. "Kotori? Hey! What's going on?"

"*This signal… It's no ordinary Spirit. This is…an inversion?!*"

"Wha…?!" His eyes flew open at this word.

Inversion. He had seen a Spirit called thusly just once.

He didn't know the details. All he'd heard was that an inversion was a Spirit who possessed a different power from the usual, manifesting only when the Spirit's heart was filled with a deep despair. And that this negative Spirit was what their sworn enemy—the head of DEM Industries, Isaac Westcott—was working to produce.

"Why…? Out of the blue like this!" he cried. "The work of DEM?!"

"I don't know! At any rate, you're in danger there! Hurry and—"

But the moment Kotori was about to urge them to evacuate, several beams of light shot through the ceiling, and the hospital room exploded. The floor fell away, and Shido was tossed up into the air. The cell phone fell from his hand, and he flew off into the unknown.

"Aaaaaaah?!"

He dropped to the ground along with a pile of rubble.

But someone caught him at the waist and yanked him up, freeing him from the rain of debris.

"Cough! Cough!"

"You okay, Shido?!"

When he looked up, coughing, he saw Tohka. She had apparently pulled him out of the collapsing hospital room. Her complete Astral Dress was manifested on her body. He hadn't managed in the end to get her alone, and her Spirit power remained unsealed (for the second time).

The other Spirits dropped down behind Tohka one after the other, all manifesting limited Astral Dresses. It seemed that everyone was okay.

He heaved a sigh of relief. But they hadn't been the only people in the hospital. The majority of the patients, doctors, nurses, and more were buried by rubble.

"Ngh… Everyone! Help me! We have to dig—"

But right as he started to speak, beams of light poured out of the sky again like a dark rain and transformed the world around them. The rubble was further pulverized, and the paved road crumbled.

"Hngh!" he groaned.

There was no way they could rescue anyone under these conditions. And it wasn't just the hospital; the damage was spreading through the entire city. They first had to do something about this catastrophic downpour.

She might have inverted, but their opponent was still a Spirit. In which case, he should have been able to return her to a normal state like Tohka and the others. He looked up at the sky, letting his eyes roam in search of the Spirit.

"Huh...?" He spotted a small figure in the air and cried out in amazement.

In the middle of the jet-black sky, a girl floated in the air, wrapped in an Astral Dress that seemed like the very embodiment of darkness.

She drifted slowly through the sky, ignoring gravity, arms wrapped around her knees and head down as if rejecting the outside world. And as if to protect her, countless feathers floated in several layers around her, forming a sort of sphere. She alone was calm and quiet, seemingly removed from the hell unfolding as far as the eye could see. Almost reminiscent of a fetus floating in amniotic fluid.

But what caught Shido's eye was not only the unusual look of this Spirit.

She was curled up, so he had no way of seeing her face or the look on it. But he knew at first glance the name of this girl. He had spoken with her any number of times.

"Ori...gami...?" he stammered.

Yes. The Spirit drifting in the darkness was Shido's classmate, Origami Tobiichi.

"What...?" Tohka said dubiously.

Kaguya and Yuzuru gasped in fear.

"Wh-what? You mean *that*...?!"

"Dubious. Is that...Master Origami?"

They furrowed their brows with a shiver of fear. Yoshino, Miku, and Natsumi reacted similarly. They all looked up at the sky, speechless.

But that was no wonder.

Although she was only drifting through the sky, Shido could very clearly feel the extraordinary air of intimidation and power radiating from Origami.

The very incarnation of despair. This was the Demon King, sowing destruction in the world far and wide.

"Wh-why...? She's—" Shido screwed up his face, unable to understand.

He knew that Origami had been turned into a Spirit. He had seen her himself, albeit only for a few seconds, and Tohka and the others said that they had fought Origami while she was wearing an Astral Dress. But that should have been, at most, the same sort of Spiritification as Kotori and Miku.

A night hadn't even passed since Shido had last seen her. And yet in that brief time, had Origami experienced such deep despair that it was enough to invert her? It was hard to digest this, and Shido swallowed hard in apprehension.

"What... What on earth happened, Origami?!" he cried out.

But naturally, there was no way that his voice would reach her. The force of the arrows of darkness raining down from the sky did not weaken as they overran more and more of the familiar city.

If the demon world actually existed, Shido was certain this was what it would have looked like. The scene before his eyes compelled him to think about such abstract ideas.

A world turned upside down, where Origami was putting down roots in the sky to make inky trees sprout on the ground.

In a few scant minutes, the city that Shido knew so well had been transformed into a den of despair that could only be inhabited by demons.

"Origami!" Shido shouted again, somehow managing to stay on his feet when his knees threatened to give out under him.

He still couldn't believe that Origami, so tough and strong-minded, could have been turned into this. He couldn't begin to imagine what had happened. Just seeing her this way, Shido felt like his own heart might break.

But he couldn't afford to let his shock get the better of him.

The situation was dire. But if this inverted Spirit was Origami, then he still had cards to play.

Tohka and the other Spirits were probably thinking the same thing. Nodding slightly, they all looked at him.

"I don't know what happened to Origami Tobiichi," Tohka said. "But if there's anyone who can bring her back to her senses, it's you, Shido."

"Yeah, seems that way." Shido nodded.

As if struck by Tohka's words, the Yamai sisters looked at each other, took a deep breath to keep their legs from shaking, and came to stand on either side of Shido.

"Kah...kah-kah! It is well that you understand. If you were to spit forth some cowardly statement, then I would have forced you up into that grand sky myself."

"Contract. Yuzuru and Kaguya will accompany you to Master Origami's location. Shido, please help Master Origami."

Tohka manifested Sandalphon and held the sword in both hands. Kaguya and Yuzuru held up their hands, and a wind swirled up around them to gently lift Shido.

"Kaguya, Yuzuru," he said. "Thanks for doing this. I know it's dangerous."

"H-hmph. Do not concern yourself."

"Assent. In exchange, we ask you to take care of Master Origami."

"I will!"

A brave melody began to play, and he felt like the glow emitted by the Astral Dresses of Tohka and the Yamai sisters grew brighter.

"Miku!" he cried.

"Hee-hee-hee! I can't have you forgetting meeee," Miku said with a smile. At some point, a keyboard of light had materialized around her.

Yoshino and Natsumi also spoke up.

"Pl-please leave the ground to us! I think I can defend against... some of the light beams with Zadkiel's barrier!"

"Hmph. Backed up against a wall here. I'll help, too. I'll change the rubble and stuff to fluffy cotton."

"Yoshino... Natsumi..." Shido took a deep breath and slowly exhaled. He wasn't alone. That gave him more strength than anything else. "Thanks...all of you."

The Spirits grinned before turning toward Origami.

"Okay. Let's go! I'll open a path! You follow me!" Tohka shouted as she kicked at the ground and leaped up into the sky.

"Agreed!"

"Roger. Hup!"

Kaguya and Yuzuru cloaked themselves in wind and danced up into the air. Carried by the air currents they generated, Shido also floated upward gently.

"Whoa!" He nearly flipped over at the unfamiliar sensation but managed to keep his balance somehow.

The Yamai sisters laughed out loud.

"You fly unexpectedly well, Shido."

"Praise. You're very good at this."

"Well, thanks," he replied, sweat springing up on his forehead; the way they spoke sounded like they were humoring a small child.

Of course, they couldn't just sit there chatting forever. Flying toward Origami in the sky, Shido and the Spirits had apparently been determined to be a threat. The countless, inorganic black feathers that drifted in regular patterns around the curled-up girl abruptly changed trajectory in response to their approach and turned tip-first in the direction of Shido's party.

And from those tips, beams of ebony light shot forth all at once.

"Ngh!"

This mass of darkness contained a far more concentrated power than the "rain" pouring down around them. Naturally, Shido wouldn't get off unharmed if he took a direct hit, but the Yamai sisters were in just as much trouble as they were wearing only a limited manifestation of their Astral Dress.

"Aaaaaaaaaaaaaaah!" Tohka raised a fierce battle cry at the head of their procession, and her sword flashed. A slice of Spirit power shot out, tracing the arc of her blade and cutting down the oncoming attack.

"Tohka!" Shido cried.

"Hurry and go while I keep it at bay! I can't hold on for long!" She brandished her sword once more, a grimace on her face.

When he looked closely, he saw that her Astral Dress had been ripped in several places, and painful cuts marked her skin.

Even for Tohka, who had manifested her complete Astral Dress, the power balance was impossibly skewed in favor of Origami. Not to mention the fact that Tohka's injuries from the previous fight with

Origami still hadn't healed. The situation definitely did not allow room for error.

"…!"

Shido screwed up his face unconsciously. But then he shook his head and called out, "Kaguya! Yuzuru! Let's go!"

Of course he was shaken by the harrowing sight of Tohka struggling despite fighting at full strength. Of course it pained him to leave this to her and go on without her.

But even so, he had to keep moving forward. He had to turn Origami back into Origami as soon as possible. That was the only way he could pay the Spirits back for their help.

"We fly!"

"Acknowledgment. Let's go."

Sensing his resolve, the Yamai sisters nodded without a hint of hesitation. They twisted around in the sky to swoop out from behind Tohka's shadow and race toward Origami at tremendous speed.

"I can't have you doing that," came a voice abruptly from behind. "Do not blunder into this hard-won inversion."

A slicing attack flew up at them from below. The wind barrier around Shido came undone, and he was tossed out into the sky.

"Ngh?!"

"Shido!"

"Rescue. Raphael. El Na'ash!"

The feeling of buoyancy was fleeting. The pendulum Yuzuru swung out from immediately above wrapped Shido in wind once more.

But that didn't lessen the danger of the situation they were in. Scowling, Shido glared at the owner of the voice, who had appeared out of nowhere.

"Ellen…Mathers!"

Before them stood the familiar DEM Wizard clad in a platinum CR unit.

"It's been a while, hmm, Shido Itsuka?" she said.

"I actually never wanted to see you again if I could help it," he replied venomously.

But Ellen paid this no mind whatsoever as she glanced back at Origami curled up in the sky. "It's a marvelous inversion. On par with that of Princess. Ike will no doubt be delighted."

"…! You can go to hell!" he snarled. "I'll never let you bastards have Origami!"

"You are merely howling in vain here," Ellen told him. "Be good and—"

"Unnnyaaaaah!"

A loud cry rang out—Kaguya.

Having manifested her enormous lance-shaped Angel, she was charging Ellen at blistering speed.

Naturally, given that she was currently only able to wield a limited amount of her power, Kaguya was no match for Ellen. And indeed, her charge was easily defeated by the laser blade in Ellen's hands.

"Tch!" Kaguya clicked her tongue.

But the Angel's abrupt blow succeeded in creating the tiniest of openings against the most powerful Wizard.

"Yuzuru!" Kaguya called.

"Concord. Hup!" Yuzuru spun around in the air the second Kaguya spoke, making it seem like she had known beforehand about her sister's surprise attack.

Shido, held up by Yuzuru's pendulum, shot out toward Origami.

"Hngh?!" he cried.

A sudden gravitational force pressed down on him, and for a second, his consciousness threatened to leave him. He bit the inside of his cheeks to keep his wits about him. He couldn't let this chance, which Kaguya and Yuzuru had paid for in blood, slip away.

He advanced with the force of the wind and closed in on Origami.

A curious buoyancy enveloped him. It was an odd sensation, like gravity had been temporarily suspended, but in a different way from when he'd been lifted by the Yamais' wind.

He frowned at this sensation, feeling like he had wandered into a new world. But he quickly remembered what he was there to do.

"Origami!" he shouted, grabbing onto the shoulders of the girl before him, who was curled into a ball, clutching her knees to her chest.

But he got no reaction.

"Origami, it's me! It's Shido! Can you hear me?!"

Shaking her shoulders had the same results. She remained limp and motionless, like she couldn't hear anything in the outside world.

This was clearly not normal. What on earth could have happened to Origami for her to change this much? Shido scowled and gritted his teeth.

But he didn't have the luxury of time. Everyone had fought so hard to get him this far. He desperately racked his brain to try and find a way to break through.

"…! Right!"

He remembered the last time he'd been face-to-face with an inverted Spirit.

A few months ago, Tohka had inverted just like Origami. She'd forgotten not only the existence of her friends, but even her own name. She had very literally been like a different person. The method Shido had used to bring her back to her original state had miraculously been the same process he used to seal a Spirit.

In other words, a kiss.

He wasn't certain he could seal her Spirit power. But it was maybe possible for him to at least bring her mind back from wherever it had gone, like he had with Tohka.

"…Hoookay…!"

He was in a race against time. He resolved himself, touched Origami's head with a hand, and lifted her downturned face.

"…!"

He felt like someone had reached into his chest and grabbed his heart. He froze in place.

The reason was simple. It was Origami's face.

It wasn't that it was different from how he remembered her. Before him was a girl's beautiful, doll-like face. But the expression on it…

"Ori...gami...?" he said, stunned.

Eyes with no light in them. Cheeks ravaged by tears. Dry and cracked lips. A lifeless face, as though it had witnessed every kind of despair the world had to offer. An outsider looking in on this situation would no doubt have mistaken her for a corpse.

Shido instinctively guessed that whatever had happened to Origami, there was no coming back from it.

"H-hey... Origami...," he said, his voice devoid of strength.

The curious buoyancy enveloping his body dropped toward the ground, like it had suddenly remembered the existence of gravity. Like it had guessed that Shido's spirit had been broken.

"Ungh! Aaaaaaaaaaaah?!" He plunged straight down and slammed into the ground. "Hyangh!"

The violent impact brought intense pain, and he couldn't move. His consciousness faded, and for a minute, he couldn't breathe.

But before too long, he felt a sensation other than pain. An incredible, incandescent heat that made him want to scream.

However, the fire was not burning his body up. This was the healing flame gifted to him by Kotori, the Spirit of the blaze.

Enduring that burning sensation, Shido gritted his teeth and sat up, breathing heavily.

The lacerations, the broken bones, and the punctured organs were all healed. After taking a few deep breaths to calm himself, Shido put a hand to his forehead.

"...!"

The look on Origami's face was seared into his brain; he couldn't stop seeing it. Lifeless eyes filled with a deep, deep darkness. It wasn't hopelessness or malice. There was nothing in there anymore. The stark emptiness in her expression made it clear she'd thrown away everything she had inside her.

Shido didn't know what he could possibly say to Origami.

"Dammit!"

But he shook his head vigorously, as if to reject the resignation that flitted through his heart. The moment he gave up, Origami's every-thing would end. The Origami whom Shido knew would never return. And that alone he absolutely could not accept.

He would not lose this awkward girl who was always unflappable and frank, who very much did not get along with Tohka, who over-did every little thing she put her mind to, who endlessly bewildered Shido.

He took a deep breath as if to calm his mind and lifted his head.

Origami was still drifting through the sky, curled up in the fetal position. And around her, Tohka, the Yamai sisters, the many feath-ers, and Ellen were waging a fierce and chaotic battle.

What could he do? There was no clear answer. But the one thing that was clear was that he had to do whatever it took to reach Origami one more time.

But the moment he was about to step out once again, several feathers in the sky above turned their tips toward him.

"Wha—?!"

He gasped. A million images raced through his mind. How exactly could he defend against the attack? Materialize Sandalphon and knock the feathers down? Or create a shield with Zadkiel? Or maybe he could lean on the healing ability Kotori had given him and just live through it? All kinds of ideas popped up and disappeared again.

However, even while he was considering his strategy, the tips of the feathers lit up with darkness, aimed squarely at Shido, and were about to launch an attack.

"Ngh!" He braced himself for the attack to come.

But the expected attack never materialized.

An instant before the feathers released their beams of dark light, a blast of magic raced in from the right and sent the feathers flying.

"What the…?" He looked over and saw an enormous airship some-how managing to maintain its battered frame with a Territory.

"*Fraxinus*?!" he cried out automatically.

Yes. Floating there was the very *Fraxinus* that had been half destroyed in the earlier battle with the DEM ship.

"*So you* are *out here being reckless.*" He heard Kotori's exasperated voice over *Fraxinus*'s external speaker.

"Kotori!" he cried.

"*I'd like to tell you to fall back for now,*" she said. "*But given the situation, it doesn't seem we have that luxury. The transporter's just barely alive, so we'll pick you up and take you to—*"

But before she could finish her sentence, the feathers knocked away in *Fraxinus*'s attack flew through the sky on complex trajectories and deployed around the airship in a threatening encirclement.

"*Ngh!*"

He heard a groan from Kotori over the speaker.

Dancing in the sky, the feathers fired beams of light in unison, easily ripping through *Fraxinus*'s Territory, and the already-battered ship was shot through on all sides.

"Kotori!!" Shido shouted, but he got no response.

Pierced by this incredible power from multiple directions, fire and smoke spilled from the ship as it plummeted to the ground.

"Kotori! Kotoriiiiiiii!" he shrieked, and half-unconsciously started running in the direction *Fraxinus* was falling.

Actually, to be more precise, he was about to start running.

"Huh…?" He frowned at the odd sensation that abruptly came over him.

The moment he tried to step forward, his body grew suddenly heavy, and he couldn't move away.

"Wh-what…is this…?!"

He grew weaker by the second, his stamina vanishing, making it almost impossible for him to even stay on his feet. He automatically dropped to his knees.

"Ngh…! Ah!" Scowling, he tried to force himself to stand somehow. But intense fatigue seeped into his bones and only grew more powerful, thwarting him.

It felt like someone was draining the energy right out of his body.

"This can't be…!" He moaned in agony and turned his eyes toward the ground.

There, he noticed something unusual.

He was in a spot illuminated by flickering streetlights, but a shadow still stretched out beneath him.

At the same time as he noticed it, the shadow at his feet squirmed like a living creature, only for a girl to crawl out.

A frighteningly beautiful girl in a dress of black and red emerged. Her hair was tied up in two asymmetrical bundles, and a clockface was engraved in her left eye.

"Kurumi!" he snarled.

"Hee-hee-hee! How have you been, Shido?" The girl—Kurumi—giggled as she raised the hem of her skirt and bent at the knee in an exaggerated curtsy.

"You…" Shido scowled. "What are you up to?! Why, at a time like this—?"

He was familiar with the shadow spreading out at his feet. The City of Devouring Time was a barrier Kurumi used to absorb time from human beings.

But its power was on an entirely different level from the last time he'd seen it. Having the power of several Spirits locked away inside him, Shido had been able to keep moving within the barrier the first time he encountered it, although the fatigue he felt then was noticeable.

That wasn't possible anymore. The pressure assailing him now was intense, like the shadow was plucking out the very roots of his life force. He was pinned to the spot, unable to move in any meaningful way.

"Oh dear!" Kurumi smiled with an elegant gesture. "You do say the oddest things. Such a gentleman like yourself can't have possibly forgotten my greatest objective, now can you?"

"…!"

He gasped.

Kurumi's objective. That was to *eat* him, to gain the powers of the Spirits sealed in his body. Of course. There was no way he could forget that.

Her smile grew broader. "'At a time like this,' you said. Hee-hee-hee!

Isn't it really the other way around? The Spirits all appear to be quite busy. How could I ever allow such a delectable opportunity to pass me by?"

She stepped toward Shido, who was on his knees on the ground, and tugged his chin up somehow bewitchingly.

"Hngh!" he groaned.

It was perhaps exactly as she said. She wasn't part of their group, and she wasn't affiliated with DEM, either. Kurumi was entirely unconnected with the crisis they currently faced. In fact, he could have said it was the most natural thing in the world for her to take advantage of the chaos to try and achieve her objective.

But he couldn't allow her to stop him here.

"Kurumi! Please! You have to get out of my way!" he shouted.

"Goodness me!" She shrugged, as if she found this reaction amusing. "It does pain me that you would say such a thing to me, Shido. What on earth might I be in the way of?"

"I… I have to go help Kotori and the others!" he cried. "I have to help Tohka and the Spirits! And whatever it takes, I have to get to Origami! Otherwise, she'll—"

"Ahhh…" Kurumi let out something like a sigh as she half closed her eyes and glanced behind him at Origami. The playful air of enjoyment around her vanished, and she continued quietly. "It's hopeless."

"Huh?" Shido unconsciously furrowed his brow.

"With her like *that*, there's no meaning in anything you do," she explained. "No voice can reach Origami now. Not even yours, Shido."

"That's just— I won't know unless I try. I mean…" He trailed off, as though his will had broken.

It wasn't that he had actually given up or that his strength had been entirely drained away by the City of Devouring Time. It was just that Kurumi looked so disheartened, an emotion Shido had never seen before on her face, and she was biting her thumbnail.

"Honestly," she murmured, "what on earth did she learn there?"

"Huh…?" Shido looked at her dubiously, unable to grasp the meaning of her words.

But she didn't respond to his implied question. She only sighed and said, "Well, at any rate, I'm simply doing what I have to do."

She jumped back a step and threw her arms out. Two guns leaped out of the shadow at her feet and into her waiting hands. One was an old rifle, the other a pistol. Both were old, antique-type guns with intricate detailing.

And then an enormous clockface rose up from the shadow.

Zafkiel, Kurumi's time-manipulating Angel.

"Now, now! Zafkiel, shall we begin?"

Zafkiel shuddered in response, and shadows oozed out from the numbers on the clockface to be absorbed into the gun barrels.

The corners of her mouth turned up, and she turned both guns on Shido.

"Wha—?!" His eyes flew open in surprise.

Her objective was supposedly to take the Spirit power from him. He gaped for a moment, unable to comprehend what she was doing.

But he didn't have the luxury of time. He didn't know the effect of the bullets she had loaded into the guns, but it wasn't hard to imagine that they would be bad news for Shido.

He clenched his jaw and tried to force his body to move, to escape, even if it meant crawling along the ground.

"Ori…gami…!"

He couldn't be shot here. He had to rise up into the sky again to save Origami.

But Kurumi's voice rang out, as if sneering at his resolve. "Did I not tell you? There is no point now in anything you do."

At the same time, she pulled a trigger. The hammer fell, and a single bullet was fired.

The concentrated darkness of the bullet traced a black trajectory through the air and plunged into Shido's back as he desperately tried to flee.

"Ngh?!"

A look of anguish rose up onto his face, and then he quickly furrowed his brow at the discrepancy he noticed immediately.

He had taken a direct hit from the bullet, and yet he felt absolutely no pain.

For a second, he thought Kotori's healing ability had activated, but it couldn't be that because he also didn't feel the incandescent heat that always accompanied his body knitting itself back together. And his time didn't appear to be rewinding or fast-forwarding or stopping. If nothing else, he couldn't spot any changes from before he was hit with the bullet.

"Kurumi...? What exactly are you up to?" He looked back at her suspiciously.

A bewitching smile spread across her face as she put her finger on the trigger of the other gun. "Hee-hee-hee! Yes, let's see. If I were to put it into the words you all use..."

Here, she grinned broadly.

"Now then, shall we begin our date?"

She pulled the trigger.

"...?!"

The inky-black bullet plunged into his forehead. Just like with the other bullet, he felt no pain from the impact.

But.

"Ungh... Ah...?"

The moment the bullet hit his head, Shido felt an odd sensation, like his entire body had transformed into a gel-like substance, been dumped into a mixer, and whipped up at the highest setting.

He lost his balance; he no longer knew which way was up and which was down. Next, all sensory information faded, as though even his mind was being diced up, and he passed out.

After plunging into total darkness, his consciousness slowly returned.

The first thing he felt was heat.

But it wasn't an intense heat like that of Kotori's flames. It felt more like he was being roasted by a distant and not particularly hot fire.

"...?"

A few seconds later, he cracked open his eyes.

"...!"

And quickly closed them again.

The reason was simple. The moment he lifted his eyelids, his field of vision had been filled with a dazzling light that burned his eyes that had gotten accustomed to darkness.

"Wh-what...?" Perplexed, he let his thoughts race. What exactly was that light?

For a moment, he thought that after Kurumi shot him and he lost consciousness, he had maybe been taken to the hospital or one of Ratatoskr's underground facilities, where he was lying on an operating table or something now.

But he quickly realized that this was incorrect.

He heard the chirping of insects.

"Cicadas?" He frowned, and this time, with one hand held up as a shade against the dazzling light, he fully opened his eyes.

And discovered that he was outside. Lying in the middle of the road. On top of that, the sun was shining brilliantly in the sky, brightly illuminating the area around him.

"Huh...? Uh?" He sat up and whirled his head around to take in his surroundings. He wondered if dawn had come while he'd been passed out. But no.

The world he was currently in was obviously different.

"Why...is the city not totally wrecked?" he asked, dazed.

The city so thoroughly destroyed by Origami had been restored.

Frowning dubiously, he looked around again more intently.

He was lying on a road with few passersby. And not because the lighting in the area was bad—the sun poured down on every nook and cranny of the road. It was a little too hot, almost like the middle of summer.

Shido remembered his earlier realization, how he could hear all these different types of cicada songs. Not to mention, the trees in the distance were lush and green, and everyone walking around was in short sleeves.

"What is even going on?" He flapped the front of his sweat-soaked shirt to send a breeze over himself, a baffled expression on his face.

It was just like— No, it *was* summer.

Weird. Something strange was clearly happening. He put a hand on his forehead and tried to think.

If he was remembering right, it was currently November. The leaves were nearly done changing color, and winter was drawing near.

But everything he saw pointed to it being midsummer no matter how he looked at it.

"Wait. More importantly." He shook his head from side to side.

This season change was definitely a serious issue, an issue he couldn't ignore, to be sure. But there was something else he needed to check on first.

Naturally, he was thinking about Tohka, Origami, and the other Spirits.

"Tohka! Origami!" he yelled as he staggered to his feet.

But he got no answer.

"Kotori! Yoshino! Natsumi! Miku! Kaguya! Yuzuru! …Kurumi! Anyone! Are you there?" he shouted, but no one appeared in response to his call.

His shouts did seem to make people notice his presence, however, and the passersby shot him dubious looks.

"Dammit! What the hell is going on here?!" He clenched a hand into a fist and punched the cinder-block wall alongside the road in his frustration.

If he had felt no pain in his hand, he might have been able to laugh this all off as a dream. But his hand quickly communicated a throbbing ache from the act of punching concrete.

"Hngh…"

So then did that mean the world he'd seen before was a dream? Had the whole preposterous incident of Origami turning into a Spirit happened only inside his head? Although he knew this couldn't have been the case, he was forced to ponder this possibility before dismissing it again.

What exactly was this place? Where was everyone? Why had even the season changed?

He did not understand any of what was happening to him.

"Ngh."

But he wouldn't find the answers he needed by standing in the middle of the road.

He started walking on unsteady legs in a quest for information.

Before too long, he came out into an open space, a wide main street. A variety of shops were lined up on either side of it, and any number of people were coming and going.

"This is..." He frowned. He felt like he'd seen this street before. "This is Tengu...right?"

It was without a doubt the city of Tengu. This was a street he had gone down any number of times. But it was...weird. Something was off.

This should have been a familiar sight, but it didn't quite match his memory of it somehow. But it wasn't as though he paid attention to every little detail as he walked around town every day, so he couldn't say specifically what was wrong. But there was something off about it, like he had wandered into a parallel world that was a copy of his own world.

Fumbling around for what was producing this discrepancy between memory and reality, Shido proceeded down the road, looking closely at everything around him.

"Whoa!"

"Eep!"

Because he was whirling his head around to take everything in as he explored, he bumped into a woman walking toward him. She fell spectacularly onto her backside, and the day planner in her hand fell to the ground.

"I-I'm sorry. I wasn't watching!" he said hurriedly.

"Oh! No, I'm the one who should apologize." The woman stood up immediately and bowed.

Shido bent over to pick up the fallen planner and was about to hand it back to the woman. But then his whole body froze.

Because he had seen this small woman in glasses before.

"T-Tama?"

Yes. Standing there was his own homeroom teacher, Tamae Okamine.

"Uh?" But Tama only opened her eyes wide in surprise. "How...how do you know my name?" She tilted her head curiously to one side.

"Huh?" Shido was baffled. "Uh, what are you talking about? It's me. Shido Itsuka."

"Umm..." Tama thought for a moment, and then her eyes flew open like she had abruptly realized something as her cheeks reddened. "I-is this, you know...? Are you hitting on me?"

"Wha?" He frowned, but Tama appeared to pay this no mind. She continued bashfully.

"Wow, so this kind of thing does really happen, hmm? Hee-hee-hee! And now I'm blushing. Oh! How old are you anyway? I'm often mistaken for being underage, but I'm actually twenty-four, you know?"

"Um. You can't go around lying about your age," he said, rolling his eyes as a bead of sweat rolled down his cheek. Raizen High School's famed teacher Tama was a virgin at the critical juncture of twenty-nine years old. Everyone in class knew this.

"Hmph!" Her face grew stern. "What are you—?! I am not lying about my age! How rude!"

"No, come on," he protested. "I know you're twenty-nine—"

"You should really drop this! I've had enough! Please give me my planner back!" Tama yanked the book out of his hand. And then she opened it up again, grumbling all the while, dropped her eyes to it, and started walking, half pushing Shido out of the way. "Honestly! That's an incredibly rude way to talk to a woman you just met."

"...!"

As she passed him, Shido caught sight of the date in her open planner, and his eyes grew as wide as saucers.

"Huh?!" he cried out suddenly in confusion.

"Wh-what is it?" Tama turned a skeptical eye on him.

But he wasn't concerned about that now. A single point occupied his mind—the numbers printed in the notebook.

"I-I'm sorry," he said. "Is that… Is that today's page?"

"Errr…? What are you talking about? Of course it is?" Tama frowned as she opened the notebook wider and showed it to him.

He brought his face in close and stared at the date printed on the page hard enough to burn a hole in it.

"Five years ago…?" he muttered, stunned.

The date on the page was five years in the past.

To be continued.

Afterword

Hello there. My favorite Lost Ship is Rag'd Mezegis. This is Koushi Tachibana.

And so we are finally at Volume 10. We've made the leap to double digits. And having come this far, the cover is Origami. Volume 1 was Tohka, and Volume 10 is Origami. Quite interesting, don't you think?

The Origami volume has arrived at last. This story is an episode I plotted out in the earliest days of *Date*, so I had a lot of fun writing it after waiting so long. Origami goes hard, and she's so cool right from the cover. The concept for her Astral Dress was Angel plus wedding dress. Tsunako provided some wonderful illustrations yet again. But Origami in a wedding dress... That's an image that feels a bit wicked somehow. Oh! This has nothing to do with anything, but there was this case I heard about where a marriage registration was submitted, the family register was falsified, and this person ended up married to someone they didn't know without their knowledge. How frightening. You really have to be careful with these things. Although, that random story has nothing to do with anything here.

Now then, I have a bit more space for the afterword this time, and to match that, I have plenty of notifications and announcements, so I'd like to go through them in order of earliest to latest.

Volume 0
First, above all else, this.

At the same time as this volume goes on sale, the May issue of *Dragon Magazine* is also being released with *Date A Live*, Vol. 0, Ver. 2.0!

This is a special edition that collects the *Date A Live*, Vol. 0 booklet distributed previously to a thousand people, together with the short stories distributed at other events! If you miss this chance, it will be gone from bookstores, so for those of you interested, please hurry to your nearest bookseller!

DAS, Vol. 4

Kakashi Oniyazu's *Date A Strike*, serialized in *Dragon Age*, is concluding at last! Oniyazu, thank you so much for this passionate and cute manga!

The fourth and final volume will be released on March 8, 2014! Please do see for yourself the end of another *Date* unfolding with the AST!

Comic Volume 1

Volume 1 of the manga version of *Date A Live* currently running in *Monthly Shonen Ace* will be on sale March 26, 2014. Please have fun with this *Date* drawn with Sekihiko Inui's stylish touch!

And there's even a special when you buy Volume 1 of the *Date* manga and this Volume 10 of *Date*!

If you send in the coupon attached to the bellyband of the book, you can enter a lottery to win a B0-sized tapestry drawn specially for this occasion by Tsunako! We're talking B0 here. That's a meter by a meter and a half. Please think of a notebook. That is more or less B5. And if you line up two notebooks, you've got B4 size. Twice that size is B3. Twice that again is B2, and if you then double that, you get B1. Double that once more for B0. In other words, a size thirty-two times that of a notebook. Basically, this is super huge. And it's never been seen before! You can only get it by putting your name in the hat!

Anime Season 2

The TV anime *Date A Live II* will start airing from April 2014. The new characters from Volume 5 and on, like the Yamai sisters and

Miku, will talk and move and sing and dance. The cast and crew all worked so hard on it, so please do look forward to that!

Game No. 2

The PlayStation 3 game *Date A Live: Arusu Install* will be released in the summer of 2014 by Compile Heart! Just like with *Rinne Utopia*, I had the pleasure of being involved with character and story development. That's on sale to rave reviews, so do check it out!!

Let's Party

This is the last one. The *Date* spin-off manga *Date A Party* is being serialized in *Dragon Age*! This is the laid-back daily life (?) of the *Date* characters drawn very adorably by Yui Hinamori! I hope you'll take a look!

Phew. Quite indulgent to use three pages just for a slew of announcements.

Now then, this book is in your hands thanks to the efforts of so many people. Tsunako, my editor, the designer, and everyone in the editorial department, all the people involved with the other *Date*s, and all the readers who picked up this book, my deepest gratitude. Make no mistake, *Date* was able to reach this milestone of Volume 10 because of all of you. Thank you so much.

Also, that might sound a bit like the sign-off for the final volume, but the series still has a ways to go. That means Volume 11, for the time being. What on earth is going to happen to Shido? (Like I don't know.) I can't take my eyes off him.

Well then, I hope that we will meet again.

Koushi Tachibana
February 2014

HAVE YOU BEEN TURNED ON TO LIGHT NOVELS YET?

86—EIGHTY-SIX, VOL. 1-11

In truth, there is no such thing as a bloodless war. Beyond the fortified walls protecting the eighty-five Republic Sectors lies the "nonexistent" Eighty-Sixth Sector. The young men and women of this forsaken land are branded the Eighty-Six and, stripped of their humanity, pilot "unmanned" weapons into battle...

Manga adaptation available now!

WOLF & PARCHMENT, VOL. 1-6

The young man Col dreams of one day joining the holy clergy and departs on a journey from the bathhouse, Spice and Wolf. Winfiel Kingdom's prince has invited him to help correct the sins of the Church. But as his travels begin, Col discovers in his luggage a young girl with a wolf's ears and tail named Myuri, who stowed away for the ride!

Manga adaptation available now!

SOLO LEVELING, VOL. 1-8

E-rank hunter Jinwoo Sung has no money, no talent, and no prospects to speak of—and apparently, no luck, either! When he enters a hidden double dungeon one fateful day, he's abandoned by his party and left to die at the hands of some of the most horrific monsters he's ever encountered.

Comic adaptation available now!